THE FUTURES OF MARIANNE FINCH

SHIRSTEN SHIRTS

THE FUTURES OF MARIANNE FINCH
Copyright © 2024 by Shirsten Shirts.

Cover illustration and design by Aubrey Sanders

To every little girl who ever shut herself away with a book

CONTENTS

1

THE WEAVER

IN THE SMALL, QUAINT VILLAGE of Silver Edge, there was once a time when three things ran wild.

The first was vines. Even to this day, vines littered the cobbled streets and clung to the timber-framed walls on every corner of Silver Edge, disappearing mischievously into the straw of the thatched roofs. They were a menace, to be sure, but not nearly as cumbersome as the second thing—

Rumors. The village was lousy with them. A truth that had become fully rooted in Marianne Finch recently, just after her eighteenth birthday.

That morning, Marianne had left her mother's weaving workshop to discard a bucket of mop water in the grass just outside when Mrs. Pettlewhip, the young village gossip, passed by.

"Good morning, Marianne," Mrs. Pettlewhip had said, grinning wide enough to show the missing tooth near the back of her mouth.

Marianne bit her lip to cover her own smile, as she always did at the sight. Not because it marred Mrs. Pettlewhip looks—on the contrary, the woman was still quite pretty—but because when Marianne was ten years old, amid peals of scandalized laughter from her mother, she had nicknamed the gap in chatty Mrs. Pettlewhip grin the "leak," theorizing it must be how such a shocking number of rumors managed to stream out of her petite, fairy-like frame.

Thankfully, Mrs. Pettlewhip didn't notice Marianne's barely hidden smirk that morning—only her polite greeting. The woman's full skirts swished against the cobblestones at her feet as she came to a stop, the morning chatter and beat of horse hooves in the street behind her filtering around her shoulders.

Mrs. Pettlewhip was gleefully occupied by her walking partner, a woman with a nose tip like a blueberry, who had recently moved in down the street.

With a flourish, she introduced her companion, and Marianne offered a genuine smile to the newcomer. She moved her chestnut braid out of the way to continue draining her bucket then, turning with a farewell so that her back was facing the pair.

After that, Mrs. Pettlewhip's voice dropped to a whisper, though Marianne could still hear.

"The girl's mother—Ilya Finch?—she's the town's weaver," Mrs. Pettlewhip said by way of explanation to her companion. "Talented, I'll give her that. The whole kingdom will," she scoffed. "The lady infuses more coin into the village in a single week than the rest of this street does in an entire year. Can weave anything, and does it well. She receives commissions from every corner of Wyn!"

"You don't say!" the newcomer exclaimed, and Marianne's smile widened with pride.

Mrs. Pettlewhip chuckled, lowering her voice even further. "Yes, but before you get carried away, you should know that any respectable woman stays clear of this place. At least they do if they want to make a good start in this town. Because though Finch may be talented, she's also . . . single. Among other things."

Marianne shot up, her spine ramrod straight and her heart beating fast. Knowing what was coming, she started inching back toward the entrance to her mother's workshop. The doors were thrown open to let in the morning breeze, and the sight of the four-poster loom was visible near the back of the space, the *click-clack* of its foot pedals echoing in the sunshine as the pungent, herbal notes of dyes wafted out.

"Oh dear," the young woman muttered in response. "Widow?"

"Mm. But she doesn't deserve your sympathy. Killed her lover when she was only seventeen—and pregnant, mind you!"

Marianne clenched her teeth, willing herself not to turn and throw her mop water in the woman's face.

Oblivious, Mrs. Pettlewhip went on, her voice barely audible: "All the Finch women have the same spine-tingling backstories. It's why they keep their maiden name, generation after generation. Why bother with the change when you know your fella won't be around long enough for you to learn your new title?

"Mark my words, it's only a matter of time before that one joins their ranks," she said.

Marianne pictured the woman silently nodding toward where she stood with her bucket. Then—

"*Murderesses*, all of them. It's how they keep the witchcraft flowing through their blood."

"Ahem," Marianne interrupted, not noticing the leftover dribbles of brown mop water trailing down her dress from where she haphazardly held the bucket at her side.

Mrs. Pettlewhip didn't even look up. Her voice little more than a whisper now, she said, "But here's the real kicker. The ugly truth. I hope it won't scandalize you too much."

Marianne stood stiff and angry as she glared at the pair with a pinched mouth. She didn't even notice her feet sinking into the grass, which was wet and bent with the dirty, discarded water, as she braced for what came next.

"As I said, Ilya Finch is talented. There's no denying it. But you don't reach her level of fame without a bit of . . . help. Important people pushing you in the right direction. Do you get my meaning?"

Mrs. Pettlewhip's voice dripped with glee. "Skill is one thing. But it only goes so far. Now, a woman's body, that can be used to much greater effect."

"A*hem*!"

Mrs. Pettlewhip and her companion jumped at the sudden noise, looking to Marianne with wide eyes before scurrying away.

Marianne seethed as she watched them go, surprised her rage wasn't turning the grimy leftover water she now noticed soaking her dress into steam.

This particular rumor had started a few years ago. Ilya lost nearly half of her regular customers because of it. Not to say anything of the amount of unwanted romantic advances.

Her mother did her best to keep it all away from Marianne, who had only been fifteen at the time, but there was no way to entirely hide such a thing. And in the end, the scandal had mostly died.

Deep down, Marianne knew it didn't matter. Ilya had risen with her chin held high, letting her work speak for itself as she produced piece after piece of magnificent art.

Her works were lovely, yes, but also *vibrant*, intricate, and durable. And so people still traveled the length of the kingdom to get their hands on an Ilya Finch—whether it was an elegant tapestry or a simple pair of trousers—and most of the village forgot about the whispers as they slowly turned to ash in the wake of the blazing rumor.

True, there was plenty about Ilya to add to her notoriety:

She rarely slept at night, working the noisy loom into the early hours. (This also gave her the unfortunate habit of falling asleep in odd places during the day.) She was also absentminded, scattered, and forgetful. And perhaps most notable of all, intricate patterns of ivied tattoos stained her skin, peeking out of her sleeves and snaking over the back of her hands and up her neck.

Marianne loved that they matched the thick, tangled ivy entwining Silver Edge. And so when she was fourteen, Ilya had needled a miniature version around Marianne's wrist. Marianne held perfectly still the entire time, barely wincing in pain and biting the inside of her cheek to keep from crying out. Afterward, she couldn't help but think it was as if the Finch women and the village Marianne loved so dearly were forever intertwined.

But to call Ilya a murderer and a fraud, to lump her into the same kinds of rumors as the fictional witch in the mountain (the one people claimed haunted the crevices of Cascade Peak, trapping villagers to collect their bones for her spells and sending rivulets of their blood down the trails)— that was an insult.

Even still, as Marianne watched Mrs. Pettlewhip practically sprinting down the street, she couldn't help thinking she ought to have just kept quiet. Because unlike the vines and the rumors in Silver Edge, Marianne prided herself on no longer being the third thing that ran wild.

With a sigh, she turned back to the workshop, batting uselessly at the brown stain soaking her skirt.

2

THE MERCHANT'S SON

OVER, UNDER, AROUND, ACROSS . . . ACROSS,
over, under, around . . .

Marianne's tongue was pressed between her teeth as she trudged back and forth between the pegs of the warping frame, winding the thread to prepare it for the loom. She was starting to grow dizzy from the unending work. And claustrophobic.

Perhaps it was because she was simply . . . bigger than she used to be. Her body had filled into inconvenient curves, and she had sprouted several inches in recent months. That had to be why her mother's three-room workshop was starting to feel small, why the lavender and rosemary from the dyes in the next room suddenly made her head light, and the laughter from the girl working the spinning wheel—Ava, a nice girl whom Marianne normally liked—sounded shrill enough to crack glass.

"Stop catching," she mumbled to the thread in her hands. A bead of sweat from her work and the early summer heat ran down the back of her neck. "I mean it. You're doing no one any favors, and I can promise we'll both be happier if you cooperate," she added, unperturbed by the bustle of activity around her.

After one more round at the frame, she gently broke off the thread and took a step back, moving her long braid off her shoulder and placing her hands on her full hips to survey the work. It was good. Precise and well thought out, like most things Marianne attempted.

She closed her eyes in contentment when a hand smoothed over her hair. Until—

"Ouch!"

Ilya wrenched her arm back from Marianne's hair, her eyes wide with horror. "Oh, dear. Did I poke you again?"

Rubbing the top of her head, Marianne turned to see her mother with a basket full of brightly colored yarn on her hip, the curling whorls of her tattoo peeking out from her sleeve and poking above the collar of her shirt. She was currently peering into said sleeve, stretching her arm and aggressively shaking it when her visual search proved fruitless.

It was Marianne who noticed the glint of silver stuck in the fabric. "Here," she said with an exasperated smile, reaching forward to extract the sewing needle.

"Oh! Thank you, love," Ilya said in relief. "Wouldn't want to lose that one. It's my lucky needle." She plucked the needle from Marianne's fingertips and proceeded to stick it into the top of her dark pile of hair, where Marianne could already see three other needles and what appeared to be a dirty spoon sticking up haphazardly. There was also a spool of empty thread tucked into the top of her dress and a scribbled scrap of parchment pinned to her waist.

But Marianne was pulled from this observation when her mother jerked her chin toward the door, her voice turning stern. "Now, go. Time for a break."

Marianne blinked. "What? I'm fine!"

"You need to spend some energy. You're doing that thing again."

Caught, Marianne snatched back the hand that had absently reached out and started adjusting the yarns in Ilya's basket, organizing them into more even lines and smoothing down the ends. Ilya laughed, bopping Marianne's nose with a skein of yarn and shaking her own head in amusement.

She had just opened her mouth to argue further when Ilya suddenly sniffed the air, gasped, "I forgot the dye!" and vanished through one of the workshop's open doorways.

With a sigh of resignation, Marianne sat to retie her boots and then tramped through the door into the street, secretly glad for the break.

By the time the early summer sunshine warmed through the light fabric of her linen shirt, she was pushing across the street and into the yard of Alice Laskey, waving at Alice's young children as they dug worms out of the dirt.

If she was going to be forced into a rest, she knew where she was going, where she always went.

Marianne liked to vary the way she moved her mind. Studying as wide a variety of subjects as possible was a must —everything from wood and metalworking, herbalism, gardening, and foraging, to clock repair, cartography, even watermill construction. But when she needed to let out her energy, there was only one place she strayed.

Vines snaked their way through the village of Silver Edge and the woods surrounding it, but several years ago Marianne had discovered they thinned out a bit near certain sections of Peter's Brook, a crystalline stream that skirted the edge of one of the less wealthy neighborhoods.

Marianne loved the way the stream couldn't seem to make up its mind. It was half an inch deep in some places, and high enough to sink Marianne completely in others.

It widened and narrowed, trickled, gurgled, and rushed. But even through all of its inconsistencies, the water was the same clear runoff of snow from the mountain, patient and unchanging as it made its way through each variation and quirk of the streambed.

At the brook, she sat on the hill and unlaced her boots, dipping her toes in the icy water and breathing in the fresh earthiness of the stream, the damp rocks, the mossy ground.

The crisscross of vines that had been brave enough to run down the small hill and slip beneath the surface of the water glistened, their leaves feathering softly as the slow-moving current gently tugged at them.

This was the first part of Marianne's routine. She liked to get her feet wet—figuratively and literally—placing her bare soles in the river and then on the spongy bank of mossy earth. Then she trekked back up the small hill and prepared for the next step in her ritual.

Taking a great breath, Marianne eyed the narrow path through the white-trunked trees, and ran.

Marianne liked this stretch of the Wood because she could weave through the trees as fast as possible without so much fear of tripping over wayward vines. She ran until her lungs seared and she couldn't breathe, her braid whipping against the small of her back and her skirts whipping against her legs. Back and forth, back and forth. But instead of the length of a few feet in front of a warping frame, she had the entire forest to herself. Or at least this little stretch that felt like her own.

"I should've known I'd find you like this."

The deep, unexpected voice caught Marianne off guard. Looking over her shoulder, she missed one of the few stray vines and tripped, tumbling down the short hill into the stream. But she was far from where she had unlaced her shoes, where the water lapped just above her toes. Here, the streambed had swollen and dipped, greedily gulping at more of the clear, icy water, and her entire body instantly submerged.

"Marianne!"

The sound of her name was lost to her beneath the surface. Blinking her eyes against the sting of the water, she saw only pricks of distorted light and ripples of shadows that could be trees as the current pulled at her clothing and hair. When she propelled her arms down, forcing her head to pop up like a cork, spluttering and coughing, she reached over to pull herself up and found a hand grasping her arm.

Gratefully, Marianne let herself be pulled, her teeth chattering and her dark hair coming loose from her braid and tangling around her face. She was nearly out when she looked up and saw the owner of the wayward arm. Without thinking, she yanked herself free of the grip—and fell back in the water once more.

This time, after inadvertently gulping another lungful of freezing water, Marianne noticed a great splash as two long legs hurriedly waded in. When she finally managed to stand in the waist-high stream, her heavy skirts dragging her down, Emory Leroux was beside her.

"Marianne, for God's sake, stop falling in!" he said, his face scrunched in anger. He wrapped a strong arm around her waist and heaved her up. Having learned her lesson, Marianne didn't pull away this time until she was safely sitting on the bank at the top of the hill, though it took a great deal of willpower not to recoil from his touch.

"Are you hurt?"

"N-n-no, thank you v-very m-m-much," Marianne replied through chattering teeth. Emory's chocolate-colored eyes roved over her body anyway, scanning for signs of a wound, it seemed. Suddenly very aware of her wet shirt, plastered revealingly against her torso, she crossed her arms over her chest and scowled. His eyes instantly flicked back up to her face.

So, she thought with a scowl, Emory Leroux was back in town. And standing directly in front of her.

After finishing school two years ago, he had been traveling with his father, a wealthy merchant, learning the trade and rubbing shoulders with the kingdom's most important people—the queen herself, from what Marianne had heard (though, she firmly reminded herself, one couldn't exactly trust the rumors in Silver Edge).

Like Marianne, Emory planned to take over his family's business when the time came. He was dark and handsome . . . good-natured . . . and arrogant in that overconfident sort of way Marianne hated. The way that came with privilege and fawning, as well as a good dose of intelligence—all of which Emory, unfortunately, suffered from.

Her stomach squirmed being so close to him after all this time. For all her moving on, she might as well have been twelve years old again. The thought frustrated her to no end.

Once, the two of them had been friends. The kind that climbed trees together and split their lunches right down the middle, half for one, half for the other. They had spent hours together, exploring the village and the dozens of empty but meticulously maintained rooms in the Leroux's manor. Though, even with such a spectacular home, Marianne loved how Emory still preferred to come to Ilya's workshop or wander the Mossy Wood. Just like her.

Then, one day, it had all gone wrong.

"Why are you angry with *me*?" Emory demanded, pulling her back into the present. He scraped the dark wet hair back from his forehead. It wasn't quite so soaked as Marianne's, but she could see goosebumps pebbling across his forearms, betraying his chill. He stood towering over her, his expression bewildered.

She glowered, stating the obvious. "B-because you made me fall!"

"I did not!"

Marianne breathed through her nose, trying to calm herself. Without answering, she stood and marched off in search of her boots, scanning the shaded hill with increasing indignation. It took several minutes to locate the shoes. When she finally did, she sat on the bank, pulling on her socks, then her boots, before angrily tying them off.

Because of how small their village was, Emory's father, Jasper Leroux, had hired a set of tutors from the capital city of Queensmont to school his son, generously offering every villager within a few years of Emory's age the chance to take part in this first-rate education. Emory was fourteen at the time, and Marianne twelve.

At first, she had been over the moon. Up until that point, most of her schooling had come from the books she gathered from their neighbor's tiny collections and her self-taught work that came from taking apart every piece of machinery within village limits. (Much to many people's dismay, considering she often didn't ask for permission first.)

So when the opportunity arose for such prestigious schooling, Marianne put aside her tinkering in favor of a classroom.

If she hadn't gone to express her gratitude to Mr. Leroux one evening several weeks in, that pattern might have continued to this very day.

"Why were you running back and forth like a squirrel, anyway?" Emory said as he walked over and loomed above her, blocking the sunlight.

Marianne scoffed. If either of them was a squirrel, it certainly wasn't Marianne, who knew how to stay put for longer than five minutes.

Emory, on the other hand, was cheerful and energetic, always moving, always eager. Always wearing that sunshiny façade to mask what she eventually learned were his darker shadows. As children, he couldn't seem to keep still. Nor could he keep a smile from his face.

"I need to get back. My mother's expecting me," Marianne said by way of an answer.

"I'll walk you," he said quickly.

Marianne stood, glaring. His handsome face was dotted with droplets from the stream, and he was watching her with guarded eyes. Almost . . . hopeful? But for what?

She realized it didn't matter. "No. Thank you," she said.

Emory briefly flicked his eyes up, as if asking the heavens for help. "I was heading back anyway. Would you prefer I wait thirty seconds and awkwardly trail behind you instead?"

"Yes, please."

She turned and looked for a spot to cross the stream.

The squish of wet vines beneath her feet reminded her of the creak of the steps as she had climbed the stairs toward Jasper Leroux's study that day. The way her heart had lifted when she heard the voices inside and realized Emory was with his father.

But it was Jasper's smooth voice that first wafted through the doorway.

"Stupid idea," he had said on a growl.

At that, Marianne had slowed, not wanting to interrupt. (And, if she was being entirely honest, curious to hear more.)

"I'm already on the council. Not much else these people can give me. Can't believe I risked tarnishing your education with these backwater children, all in the hope of a few grateful smiles. Most of which are missing teeth, I might add."

Emory had laughed at that. Marianne remembered it clearly. She had loved his laugh, but in that moment, it turned her insides to ice.

"Dim-witted dolts," Jasper joked, chuckling.

At the memory, Marianne squeezed her fists at her sides, spotting a set of boulders that crossed the stream, remembering how she had started to back away that day, clutching her books against her chest hard enough to dig their corners into her collarbone.

There had been a short pause after Jasper finished, then Emory's voice:

"Every one of them."

His words had clung to her skin like the moss-slicked tops of the boulders beneath her feet now. Worse, they had crawled over her, slow and slimy as poisonous snails trailing down her face and neck and arms.

"Precisely," Jasper went on. She remembered how the amusement had leached from his voice as it took on a hard edge, spurred on by Emory's validation, and the way she could almost picture him wiping his hands on one of his monogrammed handkerchiefs before smoothing and refolding it into his pocket. He always had one on his person, using them to clean his hands obsessively, to open doors, to pull out chairs.

"I did my duty by *offering* the opportunity. They ought to have done theirs by saying no." He scoffed. "I blame the parents. They should know their place. Should teach their children to recognize theirs. Instead, I get to watch their greedy, jam-stained fingers grabbing at all of my hard-earned comforts. It's not right. It's not natural."

"Like watching a bear stumble around in a dress," Emory retorted. At that, his father actually cackled, and Marianne heard a sickening slapping sound as he clapped Emory good-naturedly on the shoulder. It echoed in her head even now.

In that instant, her betrayal and humiliation from the person she trusted most morphed into something sharp, and a bubble she hadn't been aware of popped, broken by her new razored edges. It was after that when she started to notice the rumors about her mother. After that when their friendship broke.

As she crossed the stream, Marianne mumbled under her breath, sternly warning her boots to keep her steady.

"What was that?" Emory called from behind her.

"I wasn't talking to you," she answered matter-of-factly, heading back toward the maze of buildings, relishing the rare beam of sunlight that managed to push through the thick trees and warm her chilled skin. A few minutes in, however, her curiosity and indignation reaching a peak, and she couldn't help but yell over her shoulder.

"Why were you out here in the first place? Did you follow me?" She stopped walking, a thought occurring to her. "Were you *watching* me?"

A pause. "I wasn't *watching* you. I was out for a walk. Your loud grunting distracted me."

"I was *not* grunting."

Another pause. "Okay."

Marianne whirled on the spot. Emory was about twenty paces behind her, chewing on a piece of grass he had plucked from the ground. He raised a dark eyebrow at her, his face easy and unbothered.

She waited for him to catch up and then said, "I don't need your opinion. On anything."

"My goodness, Miss Finch. I see the years haven't softened you. Just as hostile as ever."

She peered at him out of the corner of her eye as she turned back around and continued on her way, leaving him behind, the same as she had done that day six years ago. He had filled out in his time away, becoming broader, sturdier . . . handsomer, though still retaining his boyishness. His dark, copper-flecked hair was a bit longer, the angles of his face a bit more defined.

But there was something else that had changed since the last time she had been in Emory's company. Though he did seem at ease, there was a hint of tension in his shoulders, and he kept throwing strange glances her way as she let him catch up. As if he was afraid she was a horse that might be easily spooked.

After a beat of silence, Marianne took another step in time with him, thinking on his words. Perhaps she *was* hostile. But it was only a result of people like him. She decided she would point this out.

"If I'm hostile, it's only when in the company of—aaah!"

For the third time that morning, Marianne found herself falling.

This time, at least, she took Emory with her. Or he took her with him, she wasn't quite sure. All she knew was that one moment they were walking beneath dappled sunlight on a forest trail, and then, quite suddenly, they found themselves on the hard, wood floor of a small cottage . . . Staring up into the face of a man with the longest beard she had ever seen.

The beard was silver, sleek, braided. And tucked into the waist of his trousers, probably to prevent himself from tripping over it.

"Oh, dear," the man said. "Well, you're right on time, I'll give you that. But you are rather more wet than I anticipated."

3

THE ROYAL ADVISOR

MARIANNE BLINKED UP AT THE bearded man. When he reached out a hand, she took it, too stunned to do anything else, and allowed him to haul her to her feet while Emory clambered up on his own.

Then they simply stood there, shoulder to shoulder, while the bearded man inspected them, his eyes narrowed in thought.

He was tall—very tall. Possibly the tallest man she had ever seen. Surely she would have noticed such a man before, with his dark skin contrasting vividly with the bright silver of his braided beard. He had a pointed hat, the color of midnight, and a deep, booming voice.

But where in the world had he come from?

Several emotions flitted through Marianne, like little flashes of lightning. Shock, followed by confusion. Seconds ago, she had been walking through the Mossy Wood. She had taken a single step and . . . what?

She looked around, taking in the cozy, brightly lit cottage. It was mostly bare, with a merry fireplace, a table, and a set of armchairs. There was a single door, besides the outdoor one, likely leading to the bedroom.

"Ah, where are my manners!" the stranger said, drawing her attention back. "I've been preparing all morning, I simply . . ." He frowned at them one more time and then shook his head, as if batting a thought away. "Never mind, never mind. Please sit." He gestured to the armchairs in front of the fire and then busied himself with a kettle bubbling in the hearth. "Tea?"

"Pardon, but . . ." Emory started. Marianne looked over at him as he trailed off, appearing as flustered as she.

Emory went on. "Who are you? And . . . Where are we? How did we . . ." He blinked several times, as if his mind couldn't quite grasp the correct question. When he turned toward Marianne, she simply shrugged, at just as much of a loss.

The man, at least, did not appear to be ill-intentioned. That was perhaps the most confusing bit of all. For they had burst, unwelcome, into his house . . . hadn't they?

She shook her wet head ever so slightly, subtly checking it for any pain or sign of injury. Anything severe enough to cause a hallucination.

"Please, sit," the man said again, "and I will explain everything. Everything that is prudent, at the very least."

Emory glanced over his shoulder at the front door, studying it for a moment. He then looked meaningfully at Marianne, inching slightly closer. Reaching out, he touched his fingertips to her arm. She felt their warmth bloom out across her skin and fought the urge to shake him off.

"Thank you, sir, but perhaps we should be going . . ."

The man sighed, as though the two of them were being entirely unreasonable. "I mean you no harm," he said in his bone-deep voice. "Quite the opposite, in fact. If you would simply sit and allow for a civilized conversation, I could explain myself. My name is Gabriel Glasslight. I am—"

"Gabriel Glasslight?" Emory said, dropping his fingers from Marianne's arm and looking the man up and down, suddenly bright-eyed.

To Marianne, the name offered a flicker of familiarity somewhere at the back of her mind.

Emory took a step forward. "The royal advisor?"

Marianne blinked in surprise, staring at Glasslight's back as he tended to the kettle again. In the course of her education with the Leroux's tutor, she had indeed learned of the big players at the royal palace. The queen and her family tree, both past and present . . . the chancellor . . . the royal steward and archivist . . . the captain of the guard . . . and the royal advisor. Yes, his name had indeed been Gabriel Glasslight. Was this man really him? If so, what was he doing in Silver Edge? She stood a little straighter, wishing desperately she looked more presentable.

"Indeed." The man smiled.

Racking her brain, Marianne quickly tried to recall all she had learned of Gabriel Glasslight. He had been in the employ of the royal family for several decades. More than any advisor in history. What was it, six? Seven? Looking at him now, there was no way to tell how old the man was. His hair was silvery-white but his face looked surprisingly youthful, with dark skin and clear violet eyes.

The other standout bit of information that came to her mind was the royal advisor's eccentricities.

He was said to be somewhat of an oddity, which Marianne could see perfectly well for herself now. It wasn't just his exceedingly long beard—he had just pulled out what looked to be a snakeskin satchel and was extracting an extraordinary amount of items from inside. Several books, an entire tea set, a footstool, a pot of sugar. How in the world did it all fit? It was almost like magic, though, of course, nothing of the sort existed. Which meant there had to be a perfectly logical explanation . . . And yet there didn't seem to be an *end* to the items.

Finally, after setting down a vase filled to bursting with sprays of wildflowers in water, he clasped it shut and plopped himself in the largest of the armchairs, steepling his hands.

Awed, Marianne moved forward, peering into the puckered edge of the snakeskin satchel, trying to figure out where everything had come from. She tentatively put her index finger on the edge, gently pulling it open—

"Sit, sit!" Glasslight said again. Marianne jumped, caught in her snooping. He laughed good-naturedly.

She flushed and looked over her shoulder at Emory, but his fervent eyes were still firmly fixed on the man.

"Oh, come, now. I won't bite. You're perfectly safe, I just want to talk! I guarantee you'll like what I have to say. Everyone does," Glasslight said.

Emory laughed and instantly obeyed, perching on the edge of the sofa, but Marianne remained standing, unsure.

Glasslight chuckled again. "I think this may be a first for me! I don't normally have to resort to such begging for a simple conversation. If you're not careful, you'll bruise my ego there, Miss! I must warn you, it's extraordinarily sensitive."

Finally, she slowly sat, feeling guilty and embarrassed about the wet spot her soaked skirts would leave on the nice furniture, and flinching again when a tortoise suddenly emerged from beneath her armchair. She yelped, bringing her knees up high as she wrapped her arms around them, making Glasslight laugh once more.

But this . . . was no ordinary animal.

It walked slowly and methodically over to Gabriel Glasslight, unbothered by her outburst. Its shell seemed to be made entirely out of delicate, hand-painted porcelain. Even its head and legs were white and shining, and there appeared to be no eyes. A tortoise, exactly the same as every other one Marianne had seen in her life. Except . . . made of porcelain. Marianne stared, open-mouthed, fascination gripping her.

Where *was* she? She leaned forward, reaching out. Surely it couldn't be *made* of porcelain. Glasslight must have painted it. But how? And where were its eyes? She jumped when Glasslight spoke again, her fingers stretched midair.

"Well, welcome!" he bellowed. "My apologies for the sparse accommodations. This was a bit of a last-minute journey. Your village council tried its best, considering my particular requirements. I would never dream of blaming your wonderful elder—Gardner, was it?—for the shortcomings. It's just the nature of last-minute to-do's! Something I'm quite familiar with, I assure you."

"Garcia. The village elder's name is Garcia," Marianne corrected without thinking, trying to keep her focus on Glasslight, and not the porcelain tortoise, who was still steadily trying to make its way over to Glasslight's feet. Perhaps it was some kind of mechanical toy? Her fingers itched to take it apart—

Emory nudged her with his knee, throwing her a look of reprimand, and she blinked back into the present. Though he was right, she wrinkled her nose at him, grateful her hair covered the tips of her ears, which had gone pink at her blunder. It wasn't her place to correct the royal advisor. Glasslight. *Master* Glasslight.

Glasslight nodded cheerfully. "Yes, that's what I said. In my role, one of my responsibilities is to travel quite extensively to meet with every town, city, and village, no matter how . . . humble," he said, a note of distaste in the word as he took in his surroundings, though he quickly shook himself out of it. "The queen likes to keep apprised of the state of her subjects. Anyway, while here, I asked your Elder Marcy—"

"Garcia," Marianne said again before she could stop herself.

"Precisely. I asked her—"

"*Him.*"

Emory kicked Marianne's boot, and she elbowed him in the side. Master Glasslight seemed unfazed.

"—whether there might be any particularly gifted youth *he* could recommend to my service. I am desirous of an apprentice or two. As I get along in age, I find it more and more urgent to pass along my knowledge. Anyway, he recommended the two of you!"

Glasslight paused his speech to let this sink in, beaming as he sat back in his armchair, one knee crossed over the other. In one hand he was holding a colorful saucer, and in the other hand a matching teacup, which he had filled with steaming brown liquid while talking.

Marianne frowned as her skin began to prickle with suspicion.

"At least," Glasslight said, "that's the story you will tell your families."

Marianne and Emory looked at each other.

"What is this?" she demanded. "Who are you really?"

"Sit down, please. I promise, there's no need for alarm. What's your name?"

Marianne stood slowly. "If the elder recommended us, why wouldn't you know that?"

Glasslight batted this away. "I already insinuated that was a lie. Please, child, stop that incessant backtracking; you'll skewer yourself on the coat hooks."

Marianne looked to Emory for help but found him leaning forward, his eyes narrowed. "You're really Master Glasslight?" he said. Marianne rolled her eyes. Of course he would be all too willing to eat up any story concocted by a raving stranger, so long as the stranger claimed to be of even minor importance.

"Well, of course I am!" Glasslight sputtered, as if questioning the validity of his claims for even a moment was a capital offense. Emory apologized profusely, then began gesturing with his eyes for Marianne to sit back down.

She ignored him, searching the room for clues. That was when she noticed something besides sparse furnishings and the objects Glasslight—or the man who claimed to be Glasslight—had extracted from his snakeskin satchel.

Her eye first caught on an item poking out from the ledge above the door. It was smooth. Grayish-white in color. Small. Moving slowly toward it, her eyes widened and she stifled a gasp. Neither Emory nor Glasslight noticed, as they were now caught up in conversation. Or rather, Emory was prattling on about his family's history with the royal palace and the commendation the queen had offered his father six years ago.

His words quickly drowned out as Marianne's stomach churned with dread at the sight of another small object hidden in a shadowy corner of the room—and one sticking out from beneath the armchair. Another peeked from between the rainbowed cloud of wildflowers Glasslight had pulled from his bag, and yet another seemed to have been jammed in the tiny doors of the cuckoo clock attached to the wall.

The objects were small, but unmistakable. *Bones.* All of them.

Without thinking, she swallowed hard and marched forward, grabbing the nearest bone and spinning on the spot. She waved it wildly, in what she hoped was a threatening manner, and raised her voice, trying to make it loud and impressive.

"What is this?" she yelled. "A former victim? Have you brought us here to add to your grisly collection? You can't keep us! We'll fight. And our families will come looking. Just let us go now, and we won't report you," she lied. She planned to go to the Watch the moment she was free.

Emory stared at her in open-mouthed horror while their host chuckled, clearly amused by her outburst. "I'd greatly appreciate it if you'd put that back," he said, nodding at the bone in her hand.

It felt delicate and thin between her fingers, and she pressed into it more tightly.

"Exactly where you found it, if you please, or I'll have to start all over."

"With what?" Marianne pictured grim rituals, séances to call on the dead.

The man who called himself Glasslight pursed his lips to one side while Emory's eyes landed on Marianne. He gave her a look of incredulity. *What are you doing?* he mouthed silently.

"I see I've misjudged the situation," the bearded man finally said. "My tendency toward theatrics and, if I'm being entirely honest, a touch of laziness has got me in spots of trouble before. I had just hoped because . . . well . . ." He heaved a sigh. "I had hoped whatever guest I was to expect might be slightly more open to the . . . inexplicable. Unfortunately, my visions are not always entirely detailed or forthcoming, and so I had to take some leaps of faith. It's clear now I shouldn't have brought you here so abruptly. It seems you needed a bit more of an introduction. My sincere apologies."

Marianne lowered the bone slightly. "Visions?"

"I'm certain you've heard of my eccentricities," the man said. Emory stiffened, but his discomfort was quickly waved away by Glasslight. "I assure you, I take no offense. It's simply the closest description the subjects of this world have for magic."

Marianne and Emory exchanged a look.

"How else do you explain your sudden entrance into my quarters?" he said, correctly interpreting their silence as disbelief. "Or the fact that I knew precisely where to put my magical shortcut to helpfully lead you here? It's an invention of my own, one I'm quite proud of. Think of it like a railroad turnout. I simply switched that particular square of ground you stepped on in the woods so that it would guide you—instantly and with very little physical discomfort—here."

At the twin looks of shock on their faces, he added, "I forget you have no railroads in this world. Not yet, at least. But I digress. Allow me to start from the beginning. I am a wizard. One of the only wizards left in this world, which I'm here to tell you made my education quite tedious, but I have always been a fast learner. My primary ability lies in seeing the future. Nothing terribly clear, mind you. Shapes and vague prickles of understanding. Symbols to help decipher and translate. For today, I simply noticed the shadow of a youth, somewhere between seventeen and twenty-one, I guessed. I knew where that youth would be traveling and at what precise moment in time. And I knew that that youth required my guidance, for they would prove to be of vital importance to this world, solving dire crises and eventually going on to assume incredible leadership, responsibility, and fame."

The man let out a breath. "What I didn't anticipate was that I would have *two* individuals who would fit that exact description." He clicked his tongue. "A bit of a conundrum, to be sure."

Marianne looked down at the small bone, rubbing it between her fingers.

The man sighed. "Allow me to demonstrate." He stood, crossed to Marianne, and stuck his hand out, palm facing up expectantly, until she numbly handed over the bone.

His strange porcelain tortoise, obviously upset at being left behind (even if only by a few feet), jumped into excruciatingly slow action in an effort to follow.

Replacing the bone in the hollow crook of a lamp, Glasslight muttered, "Yes, I believe that is where it was," and then looked up. "Let us test it, shall we?" In one swift motion, he lifted his arms above his head dramatically and shouted a string of words.

Marianne wasn't sure what the words were. It wasn't a language she recognized. In fact, she wasn't sure it was a language at all. He sounded like a cross between a snake and a priest as he shouted. But she had only a moment to dumbly consider before the man started speaking once again in his normal voice, politely asking the wall nearest him to show them something called a "locomotive."

In unison, Marianne and Emory turned to look, each of them gasping as the door behind them slowly dissolved. To her irritation, Emory stepped in front of her, forcing her to crane her neck to better see.

The wall seemed to swallow the windows next, followed by the cuckoo clock and the coat hooks, before it arranged itself into an outdoor image. Marianne, now dumbfounded and quite certain she had indeed hit her head back in the stream, continued to peek from behind Emory's shoulder as several buildings came into focus. In front of them was a set of peculiar metal paths, lined side by side.

A sound filled the room then. A *medley* of sounds. Some kind of bell, a great clattering, a horn, and a high-pitched whine—and then something was hurtling into sight.

It was fast—faster than anything Marianne had ever seen —and gigantic. It lurched forward, an endless metal snake on wheels, growing louder with each passing second. Marianne and Emory shouted as it rushed them. She threw up her arms, every instinct screaming at her to run, but her body wouldn't move. The metal beast swallowed the space between them—too fast, too loud. She felt a push as Emory shoved her behind the nearest armchair, throwing his body over hers as the sound reached a fever pitch, becoming nearly unbearable.

And then it stopped.

"Ho ho!" Glasslight chortled, clearly entertained. Marianne and Emory looked around, and then slowly got to their feet, though her knees were buckling.

"What *was* that?" Marianne asked, winded. And, in spite of herself, wonderstruck.

Glasslight beamed. "Don't worry—you won't be the last to be fooled by such an image. And I suspect it won't be long before this world starts to utilize trains of its own! Of course, it's very tricky business, trying to sort it all. As you can see, my visions aren't limited to this world, though my body is. Terribly cruel dynamic, if you ask me. I can witness, but never firsthand!"

He clicked his tongue, shaking his head in disappointment. "Anyway, as I was saying, I've been having a vision of . . . well, *one* of you for the past several months. Still not quite sure which. And now I'm here to collect you —or you," he said, moving from Marianne to Emory with his gaze, "for rather . . . specialized training. I really do believe it will be of the utmost importance. Your influence, unlike mine, sadly, will reach beyond this world, affecting countless people. As such, you really could use a bit of magical guidance to prepare for such a . . . unique future, don't you think? I always say you can't fight fate! And the more great leaders I can mold, the better. Right?"

During this speech, Marianne had made her way back to the armchair. Her mind seemed to have erupted, her own curiosity blazing hot enough to burn each new flurry of questions into nothing more than bits of floating ash.

Still, she tried to focus on the most important considerations: What had she just witnessed? Though she hadn't bothered with them in ages, she now longed for her pencil and notebook so she could write down every detail before it started to dull at the edges. Already, she was starting to doubt what she had seen.

"M-Master Glasslight," she started, but at that moment, there came a knock at the door.

Glasslight jumped. Then, embarrassed, cleared his throat. "Pardon me. Just because one is blessed with visions does not mean they can never be taken by surprise.

"Hmm . . ." He seemed to debate for a moment before coming to a decision. He crossed to the door, followed, once again, by his white porcelain tortoise.

This time, however, Glasslight finally acknowledged the strange animal, taking a moment to lift the tortoise delicately from the floor and place it on a high shelf, where it started to turn in slow circles, placing one foot experimentally over the edge, deciding it was no good, and then pivoting to try the next foot, until it had completed a full turn. At which point, it started the process all over again.

Glasslight shook his head at it affectionately and placed a finger over his lips in a plea for quiet, then he threw open the door.

The village elder, Caden Garcia, stood on the other side. His eyes quickly found Marianne and Emory, in their respective chairs and soaking clothes, and widened in surprise.

Emory stood. Looking back and forth, Marianne followed suit. She didn't have much experience with proper etiquette, but she could take a hint. The first time the village elder had ever bothered to notice her and her hair was more than likely filled with wet leaves from her fall in the stream!

"Oh! Excuse me, Master Glasslight, I was unaware you had company," Elder Garcia said.

"No, no. No trouble at all. How may I help you?"

Marianne peered out of the corner of her eye at Emory, who was watching the elder and the advisor with a bright-eyed, eager expression.

"Yes, well," Elder Garcia said, "I simply stopped by to *personally* ask you to my home for a banquet this afternoon in, ahem, in *your* honor. My assistant informed me—"

"Yes, he came," Glasslight interrupted. "Don't blame the poor fellow, he did his best. Was quite convincing, truly. But as I told him, I'm swamped. Last-minute trip, you know. I appreciate your scrambling to accommodate me, good man. Don't get me wrong, it's not that I don't love a good feast, especially one in celebration of me. If you'd be so obliged, I'd be more than happy to take any leftovers off your hands, but as you can see, I had an important appointment I simply couldn't miss." At this, Glasslight flitted his hand in Marianne's and Emory's general direction.

Elder Garcia raised a single eyebrow, his mouth hanging slightly open.

"Right, well . . ." Elder Garcia trailed off, seemingly at a loss. "Well, I do hope you'll reconsider. The festivities aren't to be missed, and you can . . . um . . . you may bring your guests, if you'd like, of course."

Glasslight brightened, and Marianne noticed Emory stand a little straighter in her peripheral vision.

"What a generous offer, good man! Yes, I believe we might have a moment to stop by. My new apprentices will need to learn the art of rubbing shoulders with impressive and influential leaders such as yourself."

Elder Garcia gave a half-smile, clearly torn between affront that he had been forced to come begging his own guest of honor to show at his party, and pleasure at the compliment.

Before Marianne knew it, the two men had said their farewells, and Glasslight was closing the door once more, facing them with a cheerful grin.

"So," Glasslight said, "shall we discuss particulars?"

4

THE APPRENTICESHIP

"MOTHER, PLEASE GIVE IT A rest," Marianne said as she swept up loose threads from the floor. Her mother was seated at the four-poster loom, but the pedals at her feet lay still as she stared Marianne down. Her ice-blue eyes blazed in a way Marianne hadn't seen in years.

"I will not. Give me one good reason you wouldn't take advantage of such an opportunity."

Marianne could think of a dozen. Frankly, she was surprised to receive such pushback. At only twelve years old, her mother had only asked her a single question when Marianne came home and declared she was done with the Leroux's tutors.

Are you sure?

She had said it after carefully studying Marianne's tearstained face. Marianne had done her best to wash it in the stream before coming home, scrubbing her skin until it was pink. Though, at that moment, she knew perfectly well her mother could see right through her.

Yes. Quite, Marianne had responded, her chin held high.

And that had been it.

It was one thing to battle Emory—she had expected nothing less. He had started in on her the moment they closed Glasslight's front door. By the time they were almost home, she was wishing the stream was still around to shove him into.

"Marianne, you can't be serious," Emory had said, walking briskly at her side.

"I most certainly am serious."

"But this is the *royal advisor.* You don't say no to him."

"I believe I just did."

First, Emory had pleaded, appealing to Marianne's reason, speculating on the incredible opportunity, the boon to their future, the connections they'd make and the experiences they'd have. When that didn't work, he had bartered, flirted, bribed—but none of it moved Marianne. She was set in her decision.

After that, for the first time, his normally cheerful demeanor began to slip, barely restrained irritation creeping in. Marianne had seen it only a few times when they were children. It took quite a lot to rattle eager, exuberant Emory Leroux.

But Marianne couldn't—*wouldn't*—leave her mother. Not when the worst of the rumors were just starting to die down. Not for the likes of Emory Leroux. And for what? To propel him toward the vague, garish future Gabriel Glasslight had in mind for him?

For Marianne knew that was the only inevitable conclusion. It was people like Emory—or Jasper—Leroux who always ended up ahead in these circumstances. And Marianne wouldn't be his stepping stone to get there.

Not when, secretly and in spite of herself, she wanted it.

Glasslight had laid it all out very clearly. After coming across them at the edge of the village and inviting them over for some tea . . .

Is that really how it happened? Something in her mind pinched uncomfortably at the memory. It almost felt as though there had been something almost . . . magical at play that had brought them to Glasslight's cottage.

Images stuck like splinters in her mind—tumbling through nothing, Glasslight clapping his hands together and speaking strange words, the walls dissolving . . .

She batted the ridiculous notion away, increasing the length of her strides down the cobblestoned street.

When they talked, Glasslight had said he received nominations for his coveted royal advisor apprenticeship from all over the kingdom, but there was just something about the way Elder Garcia had described both Marianne and Emory that had caught his attention. And so he had sought them out to see for himself.

But why in the world would Elder Garcia nominate Marianne?

She shook her head then, trying to focus on one thing at a time. The trial period to decide the winner of the apprenticeship would last for the length of summer, starting in exactly two weeks' time. Both Marianne and Emory would be required to travel to Queensmont and stay at the royal palace. There, they would compete for the official position, which would begin in the fall.

And there came the sticking point: Both Marianne *and* Emory would be required to accept. If one of them said no, it would result in a forfeit of the entire offer for *both*.

For some reason that now seemed very elusive to Marianne, though she remembered it making sense in the walls of his cottage, Glasslight insisted it be this way. Either both of them, or neither.

"Marianne." Emory planted his feet in the middle of the cobblestoned road then, tugging at her elbow to get her to stop. They were only a street away from her mother's workshop and the small apartment they shared in the yard behind it. "Marianne, please listen to me. I know you think this is all coming from concern for myself, but it's not."

Marianne sighed. *This* was a new tactic.

Emory still had his hand on her elbow, so she pulled it away and folded her arms, squirming under his scrutiny as he watched her for several beats.

He took a step closer. "Marianne, you *love* learning. Adventure. Remember? I *know* you. We may have drifted apart, but you're still you. You were always the cleverest girl I knew. The one most ready for any challenge. It would be a shame to let that go to waste."

The world seemed to blur then. Marianne's skin tingled under Emory's stare, his gaze unwavering as he flicked his eyes back and forth between hers. It took her back six years, to his friendship, his sincerity . . .

His *seeming* sincerity, she reminded herself. It was when she wasn't around that his true feelings boiled to the surface. Breaking his stare, she audibly scoffed.

Emory frowned, a flit of something she couldn't interpret darkening his eyes. But in her mind, all she heard was his cruel laugh from behind that open door.

Like watching a bear stumble around in a dress.

She took a step forward and Emory stiffened, holding his breath.

"Emory," she said quietly, moving even closer, until she could smell his expensive perfume.

He leaned forward, instinctively matching her nearness, as if she were a magnet drawing him in.

She paused, took in his entire face—his slim nose and full bottom lip and the dark waves in his hair. She took a breath and lowered her voice enough that he seemed to stop breathing altogether. His gaze dropped to her mouth.

"Your ridiculous lies and insincere flattery would be much better spent elsewhere," she said quietly, smugly. "Try Gabriel Glasslight. I promise you he's far more likely to change his mind than I am. And you wouldn't want to miss out on that lavish feast, now would you?"

Though his gaze was still on her mouth, her words didn't seem to sink in right away. It was a moment before his eyes flicked up to meet hers, the pupils sharpening.

"Good day," she finished before he could respond, smiling sweetly.

She had been so proud of herself—the quick wit, the look on his face . . .

But then Emory called her name and reached his hand out, pleading with her to walk a little longer . . . along their old path in the Mossy Wood . . .

Marianne had looked between his roughened fingers and that ridiculous happy grin—all hint of his irritation, which he never could hold on to for very long—vanished . . .

Then, with as much force as she could muster, she kicked him in the shin, lifted her skirts, and turned on her heel, running around the bend in the road and refusing to look over her shoulder again.

It was petty and unladylike, but it had felt good. Six-years-coming sort of good. And she couldn't help but smile at the memory even now, back with Ilya, repeating the same decisions she had stated to Emory.

"You've always said I'm perfectly capable of making my own decisions," Marianne now said to her mother, trying to finally put an end to the conversation. "You've said it to me since I was five years old. You've told me how much you admire my independence and the way I know my own mind. This is no different."

Ilya narrowed her eyes, and Marianne watched as they became cloudy with unspoken thoughts. But she stayed silent.

After a minute, the conversation seemingly over, she went back to her work, moving the loom's pedals with her feet and filling the space with the machine's unending *click-clack*.

5

THE TAPESTRIES

"MARIANNE. MARIANNE, WAKE UP."

Later that night, Marianne blinked awake and looked up into her mother's face hovering above her. Slowly, blearily, her eyes trailed away, peering out the window. Outside, the sky was moonless, dense with darkness.

Panic spiked in Marianne's chest. She pushed off the blankets and swung her legs outward, landing her feet on the smooth wooden floorboards. "What is it, Mother? Are you hurt? Did something happen?"

She hated the way her thoughts inevitably wafted toward Mrs. Pettlewhip's words: *Murderess. Witchcraft.* Just the most recent slander.

What she would never admit—but the truth behind her panic—was the idea that maybe the slander couldn't be contained. That maybe, one day, it would overtake the village, propelling them forward as they came for her mother in the night.

She loved Silver Edge, but she couldn't help the small, hidden pocket of her heart that also feared it. And, even more, the wide world beyond.

"Come with me, love," Ilya said, taking Marianne's hand.

As Ilya silently led Marianne back to the workshop and into the storage room, pulling a set of keys from her pocket as she unlocked a cabinet filled with what Marianne knew to be Ilya's personal works, Marianne looked around and was able to quiet her erratic breathing.

All seemed well. There was no sound, no movement. It was just her and Ilya, the way it always had been.

There was a soft *click* in the lock, and Ilya began pulling out several rolls of woven fabric.

"Mother, what is this?"

"Hush. Just look."

One by one, her mother unrolled the tapestries she extracted, revealing bright colors and intricate scenes. She laid them on the table, gently smoothing the corners. Moving forward, Marianne touched her fingertips to the nearest one. Its woven threads were dense and coarse. Thick layers of careful, passionate, intricate work.

But as Marianne took in the images, her heart resumed its painful thumping in her chest, this time for a different reason.

There were eighteen tapestries in total. One from every year of Marianne's life, though Ilya didn't unroll each one. Marianne wasn't sure how she had never noticed her mother working on them. They must have come together during the hours when Ilya couldn't sleep—a loving collection of years, memories, and moments.

It was easy to see why people traveled throughout the kingdom to get their hands on one of Ilya's works. Not that Marianne hadn't appreciated it before now, but there was something different about seeing Ilya's *own* emotion weaved into the art.

There was affection in the intertwined colors that made up an image of Marianne around age three, her legs bent as she curved her body above an overturned rock in the middle of the Mossy Wood. Marianne remembered the way she had been convinced there were worlds beneath each of them—if she was only fast enough to topple the rocks and catch the subjects before the sunlight broke into their dark sanctuary and scared them away.

There was amusement in another one that depicted Marianne lounging on her stomach, her feet kicking in the air as she pored over a book; pride in the image of Marianne at ten, helping Mr. Ahmad rebuild the well; wonder in the colors woven to show her writing out mathematics equations in chalk on the floor at only twelve.

She vividly remembered the day the Leroux's mathematics tutor taught them long division—one of the last lessons she had had at Mr. Leroux's manor.

After that, something changed with the tapestries.

The images seemed to lose some of their luster, the colors Ilya used became more muted, the scenes more . . . repetitive. They all took place in the workshop. At the spinning wheel, bent over threads Marianne was sorting by color, in front of the warping frame.

Year after year, the same thing, in tones of gray and brown and purple. The details just as skilled, but the emotion drained away. Her nerves fizzed, and so, unable to keep still, she mindlessly reached out and straightened the edges, smoothed the wrinkles.

"You see it too, right?" Ilya said softly from behind Marianne. She ran a hand over her daughter's dark hair, which was tangled from sleep. "It was never intentional. But as I was putting away my most recent addition, the one I finished shortly after your eighteenth birthday, I noticed it. The change. You've always had such vibrancy, Marianne. Such brightness. You're so curious, so eager to explore the world around you. I still see glimpses of it every single day. It . . . it broke my heart when I realized you were *working* to stuff it away."

Unable to look at the woven images a second longer—to see the way the colors dulled over time—Marianne strode away.

Was that really the way Ilya saw her? Was it the truth?

But it had been the right thing, hadn't it? Marianne's learned restraint?

If left unchecked, soon enough her constant distraction and curiosity would have become as burdensome and unmanageable as the vines that cluttered the streets and windows of their village.

When Marianne finally found the courage to meet her mother's eyes again, they were sad.

"It's true what you said earlier," Ilya said. "You've always known your own mind. You've been so sure of yourself. It's just . . ." Ilya trailed off, staring at the tapestry nearest to her. The one where Marianne's hands were dusted with chalk as she knelt on the floor, obsessively trying new equations. "I'm afraid, somewhere along the way, you forgot how to know your heart."

Marianne wasn't sure why those words reverberated around her chest, making it feel hollow.

Ilya wiped at her eyes and took a step back, her voice growing stronger. "My life is not yours, Marianne. I made my own choices. Had my *own* experiences. I was lucky enough to do that, even if it wasn't always easy. You understand that better than anyone. You *see* what I've been able to create. But it's mine, not yours. I want you to create for *yourself.* Not that it doesn't fill me with endless joy to share what I have, but . . . it's not what *you* want. It never was."

* * *

Marianne didn't sleep after that. How could she? Ilya wasn't meant to point out Marianne's flaws and fears, to question Marianne's convictions, the pieces of herself she had so carefully cultivated to give them the best life—and future— together. Alone in her room, Marianne felt riddled with anger, betrayal, sadness. Stinging nettles all over her skin.

Her mother didn't come back to their two-room home the rest of the night. Marianne had the sense Ilya was giving her space, though she couldn't decide if she was pleased or pained by it. She normally talked through her decisions with Ilya. They would eat berries and cream and sit on the floor and . . .

Marianne sat up in bed, blinking fast.

It was true, they would spend hours talking. But for the first time, it occurred to her that it wasn't *Marianne* they were discussing. Not for years. Rather than discuss herself, Marianne would change the subject, laying out plans to make the workshop more efficient or asking questions about whatever noblewoman had ordered a hundred tapestries to decorate her home that week.

Throwing her blanket off of her legs, Marianne stood and surveyed the room, her thoughts spinning. She paced mindlessly, ears straining for the rhythm of the loom in the distance, an end to the silence, a counterargument to the decision already tugging at her heart.

She didn't want to leave Ilya, but maybe . . . maybe this could be a good thing for both of them.

Maybe Marianne could go to the palace, could compete for the coveted apprenticeship, could have an adventure.

But not for her.

Instead, after all of it, she would come home.

After soothing the claustrophobia that had been building in her recently, she'd return with more connections, more clout. She would bring business to the workshop and prove *this* is what she wanted. A future here, with her mother, building their legacy together.

She would prove herself.

The thought thrilled her more than she cared to admit. She could actually *beat* Emory for the apprenticeship. Not because she intended to take it—she was already imagining the look on Emory's face when she turned it down and ceded her spot, leaving him with the lasting knowledge that he had come in second place to Marianne Finch—but because she had what it took, no matter what Emory or his father believed. No matter what Ilya thought.

Because Marianne *did* know herself, and she could do this. In fact, as she started hurriedly packing, haphazardly throwing things into a bag, her mind was already saying: She *would.*

6

THE GOODBYE

MARIANNE HATED HOW SMUG EMORY looked.

He was standing a few feet away in the street, his hair combed and his clothing meticulous, the carriage set to take them to the palace pulled up next to him, his father at his shoulder—

Perhaps that was the real problem. Before Jasper Leroux arrived a few minutes ago, it had only been Emory and Marianne. And he had been so . . . Emory. With his pure, unconstrained excitement. The way he was bouncing on his feet, grinning ear to ear, chattering nonstop, even as Marianne answered his incessant questions and wonderings with little more than grunts.

Then Jasper had crossed the street and stood next to his son and Emory's grin had . . . spoiled.

That was the best way Marianne could describe it to herself. It was as if the corners of his mouth had frozen in place, the brightness in his eyes flattening as he stood a little taller, matching Jasper's stiff posture.

"Miss Finch," Jasper said to her now with a nod and a smile that was an eerily close replica of the practiced version his son was wearing. Marianne took a step back, her insides instinctively curling under his attention.

"Hello, Mr. Leroux," she said, unsmiling.

Jasper looked her up and down. His smugness blossomed as he did so. "Planning to give my son a run for his money?" he asked, as if he neither expected her to do so nor to even bother responding to his question.

So she smiled sweetly. "Not at all. I'm planning to win."

For a moment, Jasper only blinked. Then he threw his head back and laughed, patting Emory on the shoulder and prompting him to join in, which he did, though his smile still seemed frozen and insincere. Marianne stood there, her feet planted and her eyes glittering as she watched them cackling together as if they were in on a great joke. With her at the butt of it.

"Ah," Jasper said, wiping the mirth from his eyes. "Is that right, son? Are you going to cede your right to this girl without even making her break a sweat?"

Marianne didn't miss his chosen words. *Right*. As if this was no contest at all. As if her being there was nothing but a formality. A ridiculous attempt to pretend they were setting off in pursuit of a fair fight.

She gripped her fingers into a fist and counted to ten. By the time she was done, her stomach wasn't boiling with quite so much unfettered rage, though Jasper's easy smile still soured her stomach.

Emory met her eyes, and she noticed his melted-chocolate gaze didn't match the self-satisfied tilt of his head or the pitying purse of his lips.

"I don't anticipate any problems," Emory said, though there was amusement and warmth in his gaze.

At that moment, Ilya emerged from the workshop behind them. They had agreed to meet here, as it was more central than the Leroux's manor, which stood at the peak of a hill on the outskirts of town.

Ilya had been finishing up with a client when the carriage arrived, and so they waited, both Marianne and Emory ignoring Jasper's early jabs, though Marianne's jaw had taken on an increasing tension with each one. Remarks about her mother's self-importance, her flightiness, her misplaced power plays in postponing their sendoff.

But she was here now, and even though there still remained a thin layer of frostiness between them after the night with the tapestries, Marianne relaxed at the sight of Ilya. Then instantly tightened once more, when she realized it would be her last glimpse of her mother for three whole months.

Jasper pointedly avoided looking at Ilya altogether, as if her mother were invisible. Or worse, a bit of trash on the bottom of his shoe. Though something about the moment felt familiar; Jasper here, at their workshop.

There had been a stretch not so long ago when he had visited frequently, had ordered elaborate tapestries and clothing, and brought Ilya expensive gifts. Marianne had written him off as either another admirer or a hopeful villager trying to use Ilya's connections across the kingdom. Luckily, the visits hadn't lasted long. They never did.

Now, Jasper turned and muttered something unintelligible to Emory, patted him once on the back, and then left without another word.

Marianne was relieved to see him go. When he was out of sight, Emory, in an attempt to give Marianne and her mother some privacy, walked over and introduced himself to their driver.

Ilya tucked a loose hair from Marianne's braid behind her ear. She was distracted from the gesture only when a girl twirled her skirt across the street, batting her eyes suggestively at Emory when he looked over at the movement.

Ilya followed Marianne's gaze. "That boy always did have plenty of admirers. Of course, he barely noticed. Only ever had eyes for you—"

Marianne rolled her eyes and kicked out mindlessly at her bag sitting at her feet, effectively cutting off Ilya's comment.

How little Ilya actually knew. Emory always had eyes for plenty more than Marianne. For his father, first and foremost. And doing whatever it took to please him. Based on Emory's behavior with Jasper today, little had changed in the last six years.

Taking a breath, Marianne looked back up, only to find Ilya's eyes had filled with tears.

"I love you," she said, causing Marianne's throat to tighten.

She hugged her, surprised when Emory strode over and took the opportunity to offer Ilya a warm grin and an embrace of his own.

Ilya smiled and welcomed him as though no time at all had fallen away since he spent his days laughing in her workshop, helping with the dyes and the sorting. She patted his cheek affectionately before he turned and offered his arm to Marianne.

"Ready for an adventure?" he asked. Excited camaraderie glimmered in his eye, any hint of the odd condescension he had adopted when in the presence of his father now gone.

Marianne blinked. It was such an abrupt change, his gesture with Ilya so unexpected, that Marianne felt momentarily taken aback. She allowed him to take her hand and gently help her into the carriage, his fingers lingering on her skin until she tugged away from his grip.

Once inside, there was a jolt as the horses moved into action. Marianne grabbed hold of her seat for support and watched her mother disappear back into the workshop, her chest growing tighter with every clop of hooves. Her last glimpse of Ilya was like a final sip of air Marianne tried to keep in her chest, to make it last, to use as a reminder of why she was doing this.

The truth was, she couldn't stand the thought that Ilya saw her in the way her tapestries showed. Dull, glum, unhappy. That wasn't Marianne. She might feel a bit stifled by the workshop, but she loved being in Silver Edge with her mother.

And though Marianne had agreed to Glasslight's stipulations, she refused to be taken in by the thrill and glamor the way Emory had.

Regular thrill and *regular* glamor, Marianne reminded herself when that splinter stuck into her mind again, an image of herself and Emory in Glasslight's cottage. Something almost like magic. A memory Glasslight had somehow taken away before they left his company . . .

She shook the thought off. Even if the events and details her mind was offering her from that day still didn't feel like they quite fit together, there was no use focusing on it now. And bringing it up to Emory was out of the question. He already thought she was ridiculous.

"Have you traveled out of Silver Edge recently?" Emory asked, distracting her from her thoughts as the carriage hurtled through unfamiliar fields, Silver Edge shrinking in the distance. His question sounded genuine—she couldn't trace any superiority in it. But she didn't trust her own ears. More than likely, he was looking for nothing more than an opening to launch into a long-winded and boastful description of his travels over the last two years. And Marianne just didn't care to hear. So she stayed silent.

"Okay, you pick the conversation, then," he said, the first notes of exasperation creeping in. "What'll it be? Algebra? Do you want to note every detail of the horse's harness, take it apart and reverse-engineer it?"

Marianne's gaze snapped up. Again, where she expected to find disdain, she was surprised to find something else in Emory's face. Humor. Maybe even something like affection.

"What makes you say that?" she asked curiously.

Emory watched her a second longer, and then a note of disappointment flashed across his eyes. He shrugged. "I remember you were always doodling things like that when we were children. I guess I was curious if the habit had broken."

Marianne clutched her satchel tighter to her. In it, there was indeed a pad of paper. Though it had hardly any entries from the past few years, there were stashes of notebooks at home, filled with each detail she found interesting or important, each question she had about how the world worked—everything from the path of the sun to the rhythmic operation of her mother's loom. Had she ever shown Emory? Thinking back, she tried to remember.

It was possible. Likely, even. Though her notebooks were relatively private, the two of them had been good friends. But over the years, every piece of herself she had given over to him felt tarnished and raw.

Still, her mind caught on his words. They felt like paper cuts against her skin. Shallow, but there was a hiss of pain all the same, and her mind retraced the shape of his remark.

You were always doodling things like that when we were children. I was curious if the habit had broken.

Like she was a silly village girl filling her notebook with childish imaginings.

She lifted her chin. "Yes, the habit broke."

Emory blinked, looking surprised. Satisfied, she turned to the window.

7

THE PALACE

IT TOOK FOUR DAYS AND three nights to travel to Queensmont.

Back in Silver Edge, Marianne's neighbor, a crotchety man in his nineties with white puffs of hair that stuck from his ears, had a particular interest in royal hierarchy, history, and the kingdom's political landscape. Marianne read his entire collection of books when she was eleven and was grateful when he let her re-borrow the tomes for her trip.

She had pulled one out during the late hours of their first day in the carriage, unwittingly prompting a slew of unwelcome questions from Emory. At the sight of the leather-bound book, he lit up, becoming unrelenting in his chatter and pleas for her to share the coveted collection.

Finally, with a growl and a call for quiet, Marianne handed over one of the books.

After that, they read in mostly companionable silence, and Marianne expected that to be the end of it. But each night of their journey, almost as soon as she closed her door, Emory knocked. It had started with his relentless pleas to borrow her books, but soon became something else—a return to their childhood rhythm of debating, reading, and overanalyzing.

At first, she had wondered if he was trying to take her off her guard, but by the third night, she had to admit it felt almost . . . comfortable. She hadn't remembered, until now, how often they'd done this. Marianne was taken back the way they'd read in trees and discuss the books with their feet in the stream and their backs on the soft, damp earth.

She hadn't remembered that until now—that Peter's Brook was a place they'd often go together. But now, it struck her—Emory had found her there because it was his place, too. Just as it had always been. For the first time, she wondered if maybe he had been drawn there for the same reason she was.

On the fourth day, when the palace finally came into view, Emory literally ripped Marianne's notebook out of her hands and clapped a hand over her mouth—she hadn't been aware she was berating her ink for drying out until he did so —and tilted her scowling face toward the carriage window.

"Marianne, look," he said, urging her to turn toward the looming turrets and gabled roofs peeking from behind the tops of trees in the distance. When Marianne followed his gaze, she drew in a small, awed breath.

Gold from the setting sun streaked the landscape like the burnished hide of a tiger. Mountains rose in the distance, the valley below it tangled with dozens of varieties of trees. Green, green everywhere. With the capital city of Queensmont behind them, the lands around the palace were dotted with nothing but wooden homes, sprawling inns with low-hung roofs, and steepled churches.

The closer they drew, the more the wildness leached from the landscape. Hedges came into view and pruned rose bushes. Gardens, fountains, stone pathways, and finally, an enormous set of iron gates through which they were dutifully waved.

Upon their arrival, they were greeted by a footman and then passed off to two maids. Marianne couldn't help staring in awe at the enormous halls of the palace as they walked, Emory greeting everyone they met with a smile—and sometimes with a handshake and enthusiastic hello, followed by a personalized query about their life (he seemed to have met several members of the court in his travels).

This was easy when they first entered the front doors and the halls buzzed with activity, but things quickly quieted down the deeper they were led, until the maids eventually parted ways, guiding Marianne and Emory in opposite directions to their respective quarters.

In her room, the ceiling stretched well above twenty feet, and there was a gigantic curtained bed that could have fit Ilya's entire workforce. Besides that, a tub shielded by a lattice wood screen; a solid oak desk that took up almost an entire wall; and a sitting room arrangement, complete with a sofa, a small table, and three chairs, speckled the lush space. Everything was done up in shades of oranges and pinks, velvets and lace.

Marianne took this monstrosity in with an expression of horror that, if Emory were here, he would have laughed at.

That's when, almost as if her thoughts had summoned him, he knocked.

"Emory," Marianne said in greeting, amused at the contrast of his muted clothing in the bright space. It seemed the two of them would stand out like sore thumbs here. "I think we've both exhausted our knowledge and theories at this point. And I'm spent, aren't you?"

Night had finally fallen after another excruciatingly long day in the carriage, and Marianne was thrilled at the prospect of an entire evening to herself.

Something like disappointment flitted in his eyes. Marianne was starting to realize her words seemed to have that effect on him, even if he was quick to blink it away. Not for the first time in the past few days, she felt a small pang of guilt, wondering what she had said wrong yet again.

But the emotion quickly disappeared. He cleared his throat and walked over to the desk, straightening the stationary supplies laid out on its surface. "What do you think Glasslight will have us do first?" he asked for perhaps the hundredth time.

Marianne pinched the bridge of her nose, counting to ten with her eyes closed.

"Do you think he'll introduce us to the queen? My father met her once. I bet she'll recognize my family name. Should I ask her about him?"

She had to admit, these pompous comments were at least starting to become a bit more amusing, rather than tiring. Emory was just so . . . earnest. It was yesterday, while staying at an inn in a small village at the edge of a lake, that she first noticed that what she had always taken for nothing more than snobbish and egotistical ramblings was actually a touch of . . . insecurity. He wanted to be *liked*.

"Absolutely, yes. Top-notch idea," she answered, already having forgotten what the question was. It was clear from Emory's expression that he was perfectly aware of this.

"Okay, okay, I'll go," he said.

Wincing at herself, she looked up into his face, searching for that trace of disappointment in his eyes again, but was surprised to find amusement.

Emory offered her a small smile and then turned and froze. "Good Lord, what *is* this place?" he said, taking in the violent oranges and pinks, the gilding along every inch of wall space. Half of her bed was covered in pillows that looked like a mess of brightly colored candies.

At that, Marianne couldn't help it. She burst out laughing, something tight in her chest unspooling. "Thank you!" she said as the corner of her eye leaked tears of mirth. "Is your room not this . . . vivid?"

He shook his head, joining in on her laughter. "I had no idea what horrors I dodged."

When they quieted, Emory was peering at her strangely, and she blushed under his penetrating gaze. "What?"

He started. "Oh. Nothing, it's just . . . I like your laugh. I always liked your laugh, but I haven't heard it in . . ."

Marianne sobered. Grabbing a fistful of her dark hair, she trailed her fingers down the length of it awkwardly. It was true, she hadn't done much laughing lately, but she hated that he had noticed. It seemed, she was beginning to realize, that Emory noticed far too much for his own good.

Coming to himself, Emory cleared his throat and backed away from the desk, heading toward her door. They both reached for the handle at the same time, and the side of Marianne's head knocked against Emory's chest. She pulled back quickly, shaking away the smell of him. He should have been sweaty and putrid after a full day spent in the carriage —she suspected she was—but instead, he smelled of clean linen. He must have changed before coming to her room.

For some reason, the thought warmed Marianne.

When she looked up, his eyes were on hers. After a beat, he darted them away and pulled open the door, his face oddly flushed as he mumbled for her to have a good night and headed back to his room.

* * *

Shortly after Emory left, Marianne readied for bed, re-braiding her hair, cleaning her teeth, pulling on her nightgown . . . peering into all of the closets, drawers, and cabinets.

To her disappointment, there was nothing of interest in her room. Not until Marianne pulled back the shockingly pink silk duvet on her bed.

Sitting there atop her pillow was a purple envelope.

Marianne blinked a few times, looking over her shoulder. Was there a chance Emory had slipped it in when he was here? He hadn't come near the bed—Marianne would have noticed. In addition, the messy scrawl of her name was nothing like Emory's big, looping letters.

She reached forward and plucked the envelope from the bed, pulling a thin paper free. It was cramped with the messy scrawl, every inch of space taken up. Before trying to decipher the script, she flipped the letter around and noticed Gabriel Glasslight's signature on the back.

As she started to read, an unexpected sensation—like a raw egg cracking on the top of her head—jolted her, making her yelp with surprise. Its invisible yolk slowly slid down her back, leaving a wake of cold—

And with it, the swift reemergence of memories crashing into her mind in an almost painful twist of color. A trailing porcelain-shelled tortoise, a delicate bone, the walls dissolving into the image of something called a "locomotive." Hers and Emory's first encounter with Glasslight. But not the pinched, planted version of ordinary events and conversation—the memories with magic.

Her heart racing from the onslaught of magic, Marianne continued to read.

Dear Miss Finch,

Are you ready? I must warn you, I don't get to stretch my magical talents nearly as often as I would hope. And so there's a slight chance I may be unable to help myself when it comes to showing off! So I warn you—expect the unexpected. And yet, don't let that lure you into forgetting to anticipate the obvious!

But before the fun begins, I have a few rules . . .

The note was long and chaotic, with entire sentences scratched out and revisions crammed into the margins.

In it, Glasslight went on to explain that his magic was rare and valuable. As such, it needed to be "protected." What might other kingdoms do, he asked, if they knew Wyn had magic at its disposal? He held himself to the highest standards! In line with the particular responsibilities he wielded, both as a wizard and in his role as the royal advisor.

He would be using magic heavily to help teach and guide during the next few months—for both the benefit and, he admitted, the excitement of it. But before any of that, he needed to make one thing quite clear:

Neither you nor Mr. Leroux is permitted to speak, share, write, confide, or otherwise communicate any details or hints involving my magic. This is of the utmost importance. I am bringing you into my confidence, Miss Finch. And I expect your full compliance.

However, to further ensure the level of secrecy I require is met, I've crafted a spell—one I'm quite proud of. It will require a token from you, however, Miss Finch. A simple reading of the following words to enact the spell itself, and then a small offering. Nothing terrible, mind you. No need to be alarmed! Now, if you'd kindly read this aloud . . .

Marianne blinked at the words beneath. Her mind could barely register the strange grouping of letters, let alone figure out how to sound them out.

Finally, she awkwardly attempted to recite the spell. A part of her wondered if it was only Glasslight having a laugh. She didn't know him well yet, but based on what she'd seen so far, she wouldn't put it past him. But if she had a chance at magic, she would take it.

So, putting her trust in Glasslight—a feat made easier after spending the last several days learning every public detail there was to be found of him over the past seventy years—she tried again. And again for good measure.

It wasn't until the third try that it became obvious the spell had worked.

Marianne moved the paper in her hands slightly, hissing in a breath of pain at a sudden nick sliced neatly across her fingertip. At first, she assumed it was an accident, a simple paper cut . . . until the uneven spattering of blood slowly vanished into the paper, along with every single stroke, flourish, and dot of ink.

Marianne stared in shock at the place the black and red had mingled on the now-blank paper, her ears buzzing and her heart racing. Then, all of a sudden, the paper started to crumble beneath her grip, gathering into black ash on her silk duvet and leaving a small, bright purple taffy candy in its wake.

No need to be alarmed, the note had said, but as she stared, open-mouthed and bewildered, at the tiny mess, Marianne felt a lick of unexpected shock.

Flair for the dramatic, indeed.

Holding her bloody finger in the air and using her other hand to smooth the mess of ash into a bowl—so that she could further inspect it later—Marianne then pressed a handkerchief to the drop of crimson still blooming on her fingertip.

The bite of pain was already starting to dull. A spell requiring an offering of blood seemed rather morbid, but Marianne was already pulling apart the taffy and sifting through the ash for clues as to how it had worked. Her skin tingled from the aftereffects of the spell, and she wasn't entirely sure if it was magic or wonder racing through her veins.

After several minutes and no additional insights, she blew out the lamp, feeling a layer of fuzz on her tongue and the tips of her fingers. A definite residue, she decided, of the strange words she had spoken.

As Marianne fell asleep, she found her chest expanding as a sense of anticipation and excitement she couldn't quite help wound its way through her veins.

8

THE DRAGON PIPE

"PASS THE TOAST AND JAM, would you?" Emory said, smiling exuberantly at Marianne.

They were seated in a fine but small dining room, a lavish breakfast spread out before them. On one wall there was a gigantic mirror, on another a tapestry that rivaled (though definitely didn't surpass) the artistry of an Ilya Finch. And in front of them sat every conceivable breakfast food one could possibly desire—and many, indeed, Marianne had never even heard of.

There were jams, jellies, and clotted creams to go atop of a wide assortment of scones and toasts. There were also eggs, smoked fish, fresh fruit, and a delicious potato dish fried in butter.

Marianne frowned at the myriad of tiny bowls. "Which one?"

"You know, that one. The red one in front of you. And that toast there. With the specks in it."

Taking a guess, Marianne reached for the nearest dishes and passed them to Emory. If she had been wrong in her selection, he gave no sign, only smiling happily at her before dipping a solid gold knife into the jam and spreading it haphazardly over the brown of his toast.

"Good. Now can you please focus?" Marianne asked.

She pushed her notebook forward, jabbing her quill down on her hastily scribbled words. "Is this what your letter from Glasslight said *exactly*?"

"I already told you everything," he answered, eyeing a platter of honey-drizzled figs.

"Exactly as you remember it?"

"Yes, Marianne, exactly as I remember it. I want to win this too."

"But only one of us can," she reminded him.

He shrugged and speared a smoked anchovy on the end of his golden fork.

She straightened his plate absently and went on, returning to her notes once more. "The letter or the taffy or the ash, they could all be clues. They might come in handy. Even the timing or the sequence of events. It was the spell, then the cut, then all the ink and blood disappeared . . ."

"I really think you're reading too much into this one. Glasslight is a genius, but I get the feeling he's mostly chaos wrapped in purple."

"What about the taffy?"

He shrugged again. "He also likes candy. Marianne, you have to try these." Still chewing, he speared another anchovy and stuck it in Marianne's face. She pushed the fork away, irritated at his inability to focus.

Undeterred, he tried again. "Trust me! I mean, I know the little eyes staring up at you are a bit creepy, but—"

She flicked his ear.

"Ow! Ree!"

Marianne froze with her hand in the air, caught off guard by the unexpected use of his childhood nickname for her. It seemed Emory hadn't even noticed the slip, however, as he was already setting in on some sort of fried pastry.

Before she could think of something to say, a middle-aged servant with streaks of gray in his hay-colored hair and a bulbous nose finally made his way into the room.

"Master Glasslight would like to meet with each of you separately," he said, keeping his face neutral.

Marianne looked over at Emory, who nodded at her. "Please. You go first. I haven't tried the lavender-peach jam with that flaky thing yet."

At this point, most of the dishes had made their way over to him, piling up and sprawling out from his place setting, with Emory at the center of the bedlam of porcelain and half-finished food.

Not needing any more urging, she pushed back from the table, pleased to be getting the first solitary face-to-face with Glasslight.

She could smell Glasslight's office before she even walked in. It was a pleasant scent, with hints of tobacco, but also something floral and woodsy. When Glasslight's booming voice invited her in, she swung the door open and blinked several times, surprised to find a haze of light purple smoke in front of her. Squinting through it, she could make out a circular room with a large wooden desk, behind which Glasslight was seated while lazily puffing on an ivory pipe carved to look like a dragon's head.

On top of the desk was a familiar porcelain tortoise, slowly pacing its way across the surface, turning around without any hurry each time it reached an edge. Back and forth, back and forth.

"H-hello?" Marianne said, trying to smother her cough.

Glasslight rose and waved a hand in front of his face, swatting some of the smoke away. "Come in, come in! I can't tell you how excited I am to get started, dear girl!" He gestured to the chair opposite him and then adjusted his pointed, emerald-green hat, his pipe stuck between his teeth. "Sit, sit. We have much to discuss. You remember Tiago," he added, pointing absently at the pacing porcelain tortoise as he busied himself looking through drawers and eventually pulling out a pot of ink, a quill, and a pad of paper.

"Yes, of course," Marianne said. Her memory of the tortoise had reappeared with all her others last night. Then, cautiously, "N-nice to see you again, Tiago." She slowly settled into the chair and peered at the creature through narrowed eyes—which were watering from all the smoke—fascinated.

After a moment, Glasslight set down his pipe and sat in his chair, steepling his hands in front of him, his violet eyes twinkling. "Well, how have you found the palace so far?"

"It's beautiful," Marianne said automatically, though her mind pulled up images of the vivid pinks and oranges of her room, her stomach mirroring the nausea the violent colors induced. "And breakfast was lovely."

He nodded sagely, as though taking her uninspired words quite seriously. He pulled the pad of paper over and made a note she couldn't make out. Curious, she lifted her chin, trying to peer across the desk at it.

"Yes, well. I wanted to take a moment with each of you before we dive into the . . . festivities." Glasslight grinned brightly, and Marianne hazarded back a hesitant smile of her own.

She was nervous and cautious and overwhelmed, but, despite it all, she was mostly . . . excited. She was sitting across from the royal advisor himself. She was staying in the palace. She was coming face to face with *magic*. Granted, Glasslight wouldn't let them remember it at the end of everything—he had made that much clear in his letter—but it was still a marvel.

Marianne leaned forward, trying to keep her face even.

"As you know," Glasslight started, "in my vision, I saw only one figure. A *single* individual who needed my guidance. The symbols that went along with this first vision, as well as several subsequent ones, made this quite clear. I can't say I know precisely why my mentorship is necessary yet, except that the person whom I shall guide will go on to wield great influence. They will be a leader of some sort, though I cannot say on what scale. I continue, of course, to decipher my visions to try and gain more clarity. But no matter what specific role my mentee will inevitably take on, one other thing has become evident: This individual will encounter threats that will affect the entirety of our kingdom . . . as well as spread to other worlds."

Marianne stared. It wasn't the first time Glasslight had mentioned the concept of other worlds, but it was still staggering.

Glasslight lay his palms flat on the desk in front of him and leaned forward, piercing Marianne with his violet eyes, forcing her attention back. "What are you thinking, my girl?"

She swallowed, trying to wet her suddenly dry throat, her body zinging.

The fact was, she had taken this opportunity to make her mother proud and to increase the value she herself would bring to Ilya's business. The rest would be Emory's burden to bear.

She opened her mouth. "I think"—she sighed—"How will you decide who wins the apprenticeship?" she asked, evading the question altogether, trying not to let her tangle of puzzling emotions burn the edges of her words.

Glasslight leaned back and chuckled, pulling the pad over to make another note. "Very well, perhaps that was a rather energetic introduction. Let's focus instead on what you can expect. First, as I haven't been able to decipher which of the two of you my vision referred to, you already know I've come to the conclusion that the fitting individual will *claim* their rightful place. As such, I've designed a set of tests to help the process along. More specifically, three magical tasks which will each conclude with a winner and a loser.

"The first will take place tomorrow morning and will stretch over the following two days, to allow for the both of you to acclimate to the intensity of the task and your introduction to magic. If needed, for whatever reason, there may be a final tie-breaker at the end of the summer. Whomever wins the most tasks, wins the apprenticeship, which will continue past the summer, likely lasting for several years. In between tasks, you will be exposed to various non-magical duties fitting an advisor's apprentice. Is that clear enough?"

Rather than waiting for Marianne to answer, he reached over and picked his ivory dragon pipe back up, lighting it and taking a long puff. A thick cloud of light purple smoke instantly issued from the end, making Marianne lose whatever response she had on the tip of her tongue. Instead, she gaped open-mouthed as the cloud crowded with shapes.

Glasslight watched the shadows in the smoke arrange themselves with a thoughtful and focused look on his face, but if they had any significance, it went quite over Marianne's head. There appeared to be an acorn, rising into a bud as it grew to a towering, many-branched giant. A flurry of movement then solidified into a gathering of birds, which landed on the branches before fading into nothing, their feathers falling to the ground. She also thought she saw a mouse scurry around the trunk before being pierced by an arrow. She let out a gasp as its tail wrapped itself around the shaft of the arrow and crushed it into ashes.

"Hmph," Glasslight said. "Well." He shook his head and set the pipe back down, refocusing on Marianne, though his expression seemed murkier. "What do you say, Miss Finch? Do you accept these terms?"

She squared her shoulders. *Several years?* She had signed on for the summer and for the summer alone. And yet, she couldn't seem to help the thrill making its way down her spine, the potentials pinging in her mind:

Could she be a leader whose influence reached beyond this world?

No. She would win and cede her spot to Emory. Watch him figure out how to go on to face threats against the entire kingdom, all while knowing he hadn't really earned his spot, knowing that *he* was the bear stumbling around in a dress.

She lifted her chin, a buzz of excitement and determination lengthening her spine. "I do," she said. "I accept your terms."

Glasslight watched her for a long moment, sucking on his white teeth. Finally, he nodded. "Excellent. Then I suppose I shall see you dark and early tomorrow morning. Someone will fetch you and give you the details when it's time."

Understanding she had been dismissed, Marianne stood and turned to go. But the sound of scratching drew her attention back. Her eyes widened at the sight of Glasslight scribbling like mad, his violet gaze murkier than ever. Marianne watched him for several seconds, unsure if she should go. There was something in the curve of his shoulders, the way he didn't blink. Just when she decided to slip out, Glasslight straightened and ripped the page from the notepad in front of him, holding it out to her, his expression quickly clearing.

"For you, my girl. Something the fates wanted you to keep in mind."

She accepted the proffered paper and took her leave, her heart racing as she followed a guard back to her room. It wasn't until the door was shut and she had shucked off her shoes that she unfolded the note.

Three truths will you gain by summer's last rain,
A blood-pricked prophecy, a destiny plain.
Midst laughter and dancing 'neath gold-tinged stars,
A foe who will raze your bruised, blackened scars.
But with a billow of courage where doubt once did dwell,
Amid fire and darkness, your spirit, at last, will swell.

Marianne read the strange poem through once, twice, three times; the hair on her arms raised, her heart growing harder with each line. Was this a joke?

Something the fates wanted you to keep in mind.

Finally, Marianne crumpled the paper and dropped it in the trash. She wasn't here for mind games.

It was only the thought that it might be a clue that prompted her to fish the paper from the trash. After all, despite its obvious nonsense, it might prove useful.

9

THE PHŒNIX FEATHER

"SO! ARE THE RULES CLEAR?" Glasslight said merrily, his voice deep and resonant.

Marianne and Emory exchanged a look. "You mean, *rule*?" Emory asked. "It seemed as though there was only one."

Marianne was standing next to Emory and Glasslight at the threshold of a doorway—if that was what you could call it. It was positioned at the edge of a forest, its frame made up of a tangle of branches, though it was impossible to see beyond two or three inches.

Stretching to the right and left, the rest of the trees were perfectly ordinary in the blue-black darkness enfolding them as daybreak slowly made its way over the mountains. But much to Marianne's surprise, the branches that comprised the doorway were busy emitting tiny sprays of gold sparks in erratic bursts.

"Yes, I suppose you're right, Emory. Only one rule—all in the effort of building your strategic thinking muscles. And your courage," Glasslight added with a wink.

Less than an hour ago, Marianne had been awoken by a maid. After dressing quickly in, to her surprise, a provided tunic and trousers, she was led to the outskirts of the forest where Glasslight and Emory were already waiting. When she arrived, Glasslight welcomed her, going on to give a bare bones explanation of the enchanted slip of forest in front of them—and their goal once they entered it:

To find the phoenix feather.

Marianne's books described Gabriel Glasslight as brilliant but fickle. Theatrical, prone to mood swings, eccentric and unconventional, demanding, exuberant . . . the list went on.

She realized now she should have tried harder to take that to heart. Maybe if she had, she would feel more prepared to plunge into a thick, magical darkness in search of the feather of a creature that wasn't supposed to exist.

Glasslight chuckled. Today, his beard was divided into three intricate braids, but still sat tucked into the waistband of his purple silk trousers.

"There are obstacles, of course," he said. "All designed, as I said, to test your strategic thinking skills, as well as how willing you are to plunge headfirst into danger!"

Marianne pursed her lips, hoping Glasslight's flair for the dramatic was showing through.

"What type of danger?" Emory asked enthusiastically. His chestnut eyes glinted in the light of another spray of gold from the branches.

"Oh, the usual. Monsters and mayhem, mostly. Nothing a future leader such as yourselves couldn't handle," Glasslight said.

Marianne didn't point out that his vision had only specified *one* future leader.

"How do we find the feather?" she asked instead, the first simmer of excitement—and competitiveness—bubbling in her gut.

"I'm sure you'll figure it out," Glasslight answered with a smile.

"But how will we recognize it? Do we get lanterns? It looks rather unforgiving . . ." She peered into the thick darkness, trying to pick apart the shadows beyond.

Glasslight simply stepped aside and repeated himself. "I'm sure you'll figure it out."

"Ready?" he asked, slapping Emory on the back. He flashed a smile in return.

Marianne straightened her shoulders. Her competitiveness ratcheted higher until it felt as if her entire body was vibrating with it.

"*Go!*"

* * *

Both Marianne and Emory took off like arrows, plunging into the darkness beyond the tangled branches emitting their gold sparks.

She grabbed hold of his coat and yanked, causing him to stumble. He reciprocated by doubling back, throwing his arm around her middle and lifting her entirely off her feet. She kicked out, pounding his arm with her fists.

"Emory, put me down!"

He laughed, the noise rumbling along the length of her body.

They continued to wrestle just like they had done as children until they were both sweaty and tired, and Emory had her in a headlock. She reached up and pinched his nose, and they broke apart, breathing heavily.

It was only then that Marianne realized silence had enveloped them.

She hadn't noticed the birds chirping or the servants shouting to each other on the palace grounds in the early morning bustle, the wind blowing the leaves—not until she glanced around and discovered it had all gone away.

Goosebumps broke out across her neck, both from the chill as her sweat turned cold and from her sudden shiver of misgiving.

She attempted to split into opposite directions, but before she could move more than a foot, Emory had grasped her hand, tugging her back. She looked down at their linked fingers, blinking.

"Good luck, Miss Finch," he said.

"I don't need luck."

His smile widened as he let his hand slip away. "I know."

After that, Emory went to the right, while Marianne pivoted left. So far, the space around her didn't appear to be much more than a forest—the same landscape she would have seen had she entered the tree line at any other point. Except for the oddly enveloping darkness. And the silence.

A puff of gold glimmer sprayed out from the branch of a nearby tree, rippling like a cloud of smoke. Marianne tried to dodge it, but the sparks were blindingly bright in the shadows. Blinking them away, she ended up plunging herself even deeper into the quickly fading cloud of glittering light.

When she opened her eyes fully, she screamed.

Everything around her had turned on its head. The trees were growing from the ground, reaching their branches up, and she was suspended above them. Although strangely, the blood wasn't rushing to Marianne's head, and gravity still pulled her hair down her back. But the fact that her bodily sensations were not in line with what she was seeing did nothing to calm her racing heart. She was trapped in the sky, more than a dozen feet above the ground.

Hesitantly, she reached an arm out, expecting to grab hold of the oddly still leaves just in front of her—leaves reaching up from the base of the tree far below. Maybe if she got a good enough grip, she could use the branches to make her way back down. But when she closed her fingers, Marianne felt only air.

Leaning her body forward, she put both arms out. There was nothing. She did manage to reach the leaves, but they only wisped like smoke at the touch of her fingers, and even this was difficult to make out in the darkness engulfing her.

"Where are you?" she called angrily to the trees. "I don't appreciate tricks!"

Slowly, so slowly it was almost painful, she reached out a foot, firmly planting it in the middle of nothing—pure, dark sky. She tested with her toe and was surprised to find the feel of solid ground beneath her. Again, with excruciatingly measured movements, she shifted her weight until she had taken a full step. Three more, each with a bit more confidence, and Marianne ran face-first into something.

"Ouch!" She rubbed her nose vigorously as tears of pain sprang to her eyes. Using the tips of her fingers, she reached out again and felt what was unmistakably the bark of a tree —the tree directly in front of her.

Which meant she must be walking on solid ground, the illusion making it look as though she were suspended in the sky.

Even this realization did little to increase her progress, however, because while she managed to avoid any more face-plants with solid trunks, she did run headfirst into a tangle of branches, and tripped over a boulder, scratching the palms of her hands in the pebbled earth.

She drew a little comfort from the fact that this forest, at least, was free of the chaotic vines that plagued Silver Edge. She couldn't imagine trying to pick her way over those in this upside-down, murky darkness.

"All right, Glasslight. Your illusions don't scare me," she whispered feverishly to no one in particular.

A couple of times over the next long stretch, continuing to take one step after another as fast as she dared, her stomach clenched in frustration at her slowness. Marianne tensed at the sound of a soft, eerie clinking, like delicate glasses gently knocking together. But as she perked her ears and stilled her body, the sound became more elusive, slowly fading into nothing.

All in all, she had barely navigated her way more than a hundred feet into the forest (the original tree she had crashed into was still visible) when she suddenly felt a yanking sensation, as though arms had wrapped around her waist and stopped her from stepping into a busy, carriage-filled street.

The next thing she knew, she was blinking against the glare of the morning sun, back on the palace grounds.

Glasslight beamed at her. "We have a winner!"

Marianne spluttered, wondering how on earth what she had done counted as winning, when Glasslight's massive frame shifted to reveal a pleased-as-punch Emory behind him, delicately holding a crimson feather.

He ran the pad of his thumb along the soft part, making the feather ripple red and gold, and Marianne's vision went dark with indignation.

"No!" she cried, unable to stop herself.

How on earth had he won already? There was no way he encountered the gold glitter, right? If so, he never would have navigated the enchanted forest so quickly.

Still, after forcing her face into a stiff smile, she managed to mutter, "Congratulations."

To be fair, Emory didn't exactly look smug, just delighted. He made no snide comments, but the way he was caressing the feather . . . She wanted to throw something at him.

If she was here, she would try, she recited internally once more. She would take advantage of the opportunity. She would *win*.

Whatever their next task, she would—

"Shall we go again?" Glasslight said, cutting into her thoughts. Both Marianne's and Emory's heads whipped toward him.

"The feather will be placed in a different location. You may encounter different obstacles. See if you can, perhaps, shorten the time it takes you to find it."

Marianne looked to the sky, realizing for the first time that she must have been in the dark forest for at least two full hours, judging by the placement of the sun.

"And handle that gently, if you please," Glasslight added, plucking the feather from between Emory's fingers. "You have no idea the ordeal it took to get my hands on this. And it's the entire key to the confined challenge. Phoenix feathers aren't just rare, you know—they're extinct in this world. But I've found that mythical creatures provide a certain potency to my spells that I just can't find elsewhere. The bones that alarmed you so, dear Marianne, upon our first meeting—do you remember? That was the skeleton of a pygmy dragon. Quite useful, indeed. Allows for a great deal of flexibility and variance, as well as fuel to power the spell. I've searched every corner of this land, spent more than a small fortune and a few unseemly trades to get my hands on what I believe to be a nearly complete collection of magical creature artifacts to aid in my spellwork. Impressive, no?"

He smiled at Emory and Marianne expectantly, waiting for their inevitable praise.

Emory moved closer, peering at the feather with a new light in his eyes, and even Marianne's fingers itched to hold it as wonder momentarily crowded out her anger at losing.

"That is amazing, Master Glasslight," Emory said with awe, prompting a pleased grin from their mentor.

For the first time, Marianne looked beyond where Glasslight and Emory stood, surprised to see a luxurious setup, much like a sitting room, in the shade of a nearby tree.

Glasslight followed her gaze. "Oh yes. Couldn't exactly be expected to lounge in the grass all day, could I? This way I can get a spot of work done while you two manage things in there."

Marianne didn't answer. She just took in the table cluttered with books and other random objects, the plush armchairs, the thick, woven, brightly colored rugs overlapping one another. There was even a portable fireplace. His tortoise—Tiago—was dutifully making its way over from the setup. Glasslight must have rushed over when Emory emerged victorious from the forest. Had he been yanked out in the same way Marianne had? Perhaps for whoever won, the exit was a little smoother.

Glasslight cut into her observations. She had barely dusted off her dress, straightened it as best she could, and taken a breath before he said, "Now. Ready to see what else the forest has in store for you?"

He held the feather up before speaking another word in a language that barely registered as one to Marianne's ears, the same as he had done in the cottage. The feather disappeared. To a new hiding place, Glasslight said.

Marianne was far from ready, but she squared her shoulders all the same, re-braiding her hair as she remembered Glasslight's words from his office. The first challenge would last two full days.

She could still win.

Acting on impulse, she bent down and untied Emory's shoelace. With a laugh, he retaliated by yanking the ribbon from her freshly braided hair.

Before she could retie it, Glasslight had taken a deep breath and opened his mouth:

"Go!"

10

THE FEAST

THIS TIME, MARIANNE DIDN'T HESITATE. She charged into the forest, getting a decent head start on Emory.

Figuring he had the right idea, she went right this time. Because it had to have been pure luck that he had found the feather first. If she had taken this path on their first go, she surely would have avoided the gold glitter and come out victorious. So she felt hopeful as she pressed deeper into the dark, silent trees, watching carefully for any signs of incoming belches of sparks.

Marianne had been walking for about twenty minutes, the ground becoming softer, when the delicate sound of clinking glass caught her ear. She stopped, waiting, deliberating.

Which direction was it coming from? Should she move toward it or away from it? Did it hold untold horrors like the seemingly beautiful sparks of gold?

The sound abruptly cut off when Marianne took another step and sank into the ground.

Again, she screamed, though this time it was muffled by the earth pressing in around her as she continued to fall. Panic clawed at her chest. She had thought that the open air, as the world turned upside down, had been bad, but this was worse. She was being buried alive. She needed to find a way to calm down, to think her way out of this—

Marianne landed with a thump on the forest floor. It was just as dark and silent as ever, though she was undoubtedly in a different section now. With a huff of frustration, she stood and started forward again.

It didn't matter, she told herself. It was just as likely she was closer to the feather as that the ground had taken her farther away, right?

Another long stretch, in which Marianne managed to successfully dodge two clouds of gold sparks, finally led her to the source of the otherworldly tinkling.

Turning the corner, Marianne came face to face with another tree, this one taller and wider than any around it. But rather than leaves, the tree was crowded with delicate glass baubles that seemed to ripple in a phantom breeze, clinking against one another.

She walked toward it, cautious, using her toe to test the ground and reaching out a finger, intending to touch the glass with no more than the tip of her nail—and was yanked out of the forest again.

"*How?*" she shouted this time, unable to contain her anger. Especially when she spotted Emory with the feather (looking only slightly worse for the wear), and Glasslight wearing a cheerful expression.

The sight of them ignited angry fire in her veins.

She needed to try harder.

On the third attempt, Marianne discovered the most unpleasant obstacle of all.

It was while she was tiptoeing around what she believed to be a rather suspicious boulder that some of the shadows around it suddenly . . . detached themselves from the ground.

She watched in horror, her skin cold with dread, as the shadows rose slowly up, looming above her like demons, curls of blackness rising from them. Looking left and right, Marianne lunged out of the way just as a tendril plunged forward, wrapping inky arms around where she had been standing moments before.

Making herself as small as she could, Marianne watched, her heart pounding painfully, as the shadows rearranged themselves, sinking back to the ground until she could no longer see them in the dimness.

She breathed out a single shaky breath, then another, afraid to move, unsure how much time was passing. It could have been five minutes or an hour. Her heartbeat was too erratic to keep time, her mind too numb to separate the world around her from her own stream of panic.

The silence pressed against her ears.

Finally, unwilling to stay still any longer, Marianne moved. As if they had been waiting for her, the shadows shifted, pounced. Before she could break away, lengths of black were wrapping themselves around her arms and legs. She began to scream.

She tried to pull away. She fought, ignoring the way the pain increased as the shadows wrapped tighter around her with every movement, spiraling up her arms and into her hair. The shadows tugged, screeching into the silence and making her scalp ache, digging trenches into her wrists.

Within minutes, all of her energy was spent, leaked into the shadows themselves. She stopped fighting and sat, thinking, but no solution came to mind. There was no help to be had.

"Nasty, rotten, rude things!" she cried. "Let go this instant!"

But her demands proved just as fruitless as her fight, and eventually, after what felt like hours, her exhaustion gave way to sleep.

Marianne had no idea how much time she spent pinned to the earth like that before she was yanked out of the forest again. All she knew was that when she came to, trembling and weak, the moon was high in the sky, and she was unable to summon the energy to feel anything more than a vague flicker of irritation.

This time, at least, Emory didn't look nearly as put-together.

He was covered in dirt, his hair sticking up at odd angles, his clothing torn in more than one place, including an area on his chest that seemed to be coated in an astonishing amount of dried blood. But he still held the phoenix feather, with an exhausted but relieved expression on his face.

However, one look at Marianne and all relief fell away. His hand holding the feather dropped to his side as he rushed toward her.

"Ree! Are you okay?" he asked, searching her face, feathering his touch over her skin and the raw, red welts on her wrists. After a moment, he wrapped his warm fingers around her arm, pulling her up, and for the first time Marianne realized how cold she was.

She tried to shrug him off, but his grip remained firm.

"I'm fine," she said firmly, standing on shaking legs. Her stretch in the forest was nightmarish, but she refused to dwell on it. Clearly, Emory had met some trouble of his own. She wouldn't be the one to complain.

Emory turned to Glasslight, his face darkening. Marianne could see his emotions at war—he was angry, that much was clear, but she also knew years of breeding had taught Emory Leroux one thing above all else: To respect and admire those in superior positions.

Emory's breeding won out. In a controlled voice, he said, "What sort of game are you playing at? What if something had happened in there?"

Glasslight's smile never faltered. He waved this off. "Oh, my dear boy, it's nothing someone with a destiny such as the two of you couldn't handle!"

He bounced on his feet and moved over to the forest doorway to straighten a branch that had started to droop, his odd tortoise companion—who had once again just managed to reach Glasslight's feet—dutifully following in his wake.

This answer did nothing to soothe Marianne. Nor, it seemed, Emory. His brows furrowed, his grip on Marianne's arm tightening to the point of discomfort, but he said no more.

"I don't need your worry," Marianne whispered angrily.

It was bad enough he was making her look like a fool. This was supposed to be easy. She knew he would take the apprenticeship eventually, but it was only supposed to happen after she had her say. Only after she brought recognition and clout to Ilya's business.

Emory answered her declaration and accompanying glare with an expression she couldn't begin to parse in her current exhaustion, though he didn't let go of her arm.

"Now," Glasslight said, "dinner? I expect you're more than a little hungry. Please forgive this oversight, if you will. I promise not to forget the refreshments tomorrow."

Unable to hold herself up any longer, Marianne (against her better judgment) leaned into Emory. He gave her a startled look before removing his hand from her arm and snaking it around her as she wrapped an arm around his neck. Pulling her close, he kept her steady as their attention turned to a small figure hobbling over.

In the light of the moon, Marianne could make out little more than a head of white hair on the newcomer, including a bushy beard. As he neared, the man stopped next to Glasslight, coming barely to his shoulder, and looked up at Marianne and Emory with wide, wonder-struck eyes.

"Did I miss it?" he said in a creaking, excited voice. "Oh, Gabriel, you old fiend, you were supposed to warn me when they were done!"

Glasslight shrugged, still grinning. "As I've said, good man, no way to do so! If you wanted to see the win, you needed to do the hard work of waiting, like me."

Marianne's irritation flared a bit hotter at Glasslight's definition of hard work, but she kept silent. Instead of watching him, she distracted herself by focusing on the slow-moving tortoise. Tiago was now only a few paces away from Glasslight's new spot near the branched doorway, steadily trodding his four legs one after the other.

"You could've waited, too. I managed to keep myself entertained," Glasslight said, waving to the lavish living area he had set up.

"And shirk your duties, you rascal!"

"Oh, pish. This is the greatest work I've undertaken yet!" Glasslight said a little indignantly.

The newcomer wheezed out a scornful laugh, and Glasslight's cheerful demeanor vanished.

He scowled at the tiny man. "Miss Finch, Mr. Leroux, I'd like to introduce you to Arthur Winthrop, another self-important royal member of the staff—and a fool."

This time, Marianne's mind, even in its exhaustion, didn't have to grasp around for the answer to the flicker of familiarity the name created:

Arthur Winthrop, royal archivist. Her studying had included an exhaustive list of every palace official. She just wished she had the strength to summon a bit more excitement at their first introduction.

"Not to mention his best friend of eighty years," Arthur interjected. "Means I've had a front-row seat to every one of his flubs. Keeps me entertained, I can tell you that! But of course he's come a long way. Look at the way that doorway into an enchanted forest is almost symmetrical! And please, call me Artie."

Glasslight went on, wagging a finger at Artie. "Should never have shared my secrets with you! I can take it all away, you know. Don't think I won't! Every memory, every magical inkling. You have no right to my wizardry if I don't feel like it!"

Artie, appearing unaffected by Glasslight's insult, laughed again. "Now, Gabriel, it's the same threat every week. You know I'm only having a bit of fun. I'd simply forgotten about the *visions*. The very workings of 'fate!'" He winked at Emory and Marianne. "What an honor to meet the future Mistress or Master something-or-the-other! May I just express, in advance, my deep gratitude for all of the greatness your excellencies, one or the both, or some such of you, are sure to bestow on this-or-that. Our kingdom has been or will be or may someday turn out to be, never the same!"

Glasslight's expression turned positively thunderous. "Now, see here!"

"Oh, come off it, Gabriel. Of course I believe in your visions. The last time you smoked, you told me my great-aunt would die and pass along her entire shoe collection to me. And I'll tell you, anyone who predicts the death of that old bat has my sympathy. Never matter she's going on one-hundred-and-forty-three next month. Already got the birthday invite," he added in an undertone to Marianne and Emory.

"Mark my words, you will not attend that party!" Glasslight huffed. Tiago finally reached him and sank down in the grass, only to push shakily back to his feet when Glasslight marched off in the opposite direction and started digging through a pile of clutter on the table.

At this point, Marianne, who had watched all of this unfold while leaning ever farther into Emory, officially lost the ability to stand. Apparently, rather than training her mind in facts, she ought to have been training her body to go long stretches without food, water, or free use of her own limbs.

Emory, not missing a beat, caught her with his other hand, skillfully transferring the phoenix feather to the pocket of his shirt and wrapping her arms around his neck as he led her toward one of Glasslight's armchairs. She wanted to be indignant, to summon a quippy remark or a lick of competitive fire, but she came up short.

Unfortunately, they hadn't quite made it to the blessed armchair before Glasslight, in his continued rummaging, said: "Now, where is that blasted—oh, here it is." He lifted a tiny bone in the air, set it gently at the bottom of his open traveling bag, and then adjusted a few more bones in various areas of the makeshift sitting room, even getting on his knees to bury another in the earth.

He stood and clapped dirt from his hands. "Couldn't bury it before, or I never would've found it again. Marianne, keep an eye on that spot, will you? I've lost more than one wing bone to a poorly marked grave."

Then he lifted his hands, spoke his nonsense words in a booming voice, and Marianne, still leaning against Emory, watched in a dull sort of wonder as the entirety of the sitting room shrank to the size of a doll set. One more word, and it vanished from sight, taking the plush, welcoming armchair with it. Marianne suspected everything had reappeared safely inside the traveling bag, but that did her aching body little good now.

However, she had to wait only a heartbeat before, in the sitting area's place on the grass, there appeared a single miniature table, laid out with food too tiny for Marianne to identify.

A final word, and the table and four chairs enlarged in one great motion. Marianne nearly sank out of Emory's grip as the smell of vegetable pie and steamed pumpkin wafted over.

Glasslight shot Artie one more offended look, then seemed to decide the fight was over and announced, "I'm famished. Let's eat."

11

THE DEFEAT

OVER DINNER, AS MARIANNE REGAINED some of her strength, she learned she had, in fact, faced all of the horrors within the forest. As had Emory.

"Perplexing vexing," Glasslight announced proudly when Marianne described the gold sparks that shifted the world upside down. "My own invention."

"Yes. That was . . . not my favorite," Emory admitted, spearing a chunk of roasted pumpkin with his golden fork, followed by an anchovy, which seemed to be a palace specialty. He was on his third helping. Marianne was unable to stop a tired smirk from creeping along her lips as she took in the image of his impeccable manners, as he ate one tiny silver fish after another, the smudges of dirt on his face and blood on his clothing offering the scene an edge of added absurdity.

Then there were the two additional enchantments, making three obstacles in total: the enchanted earth—which whisked them into different parts of the forest—and the shadow stalkers—which Marianne hoped to never encounter again.

"No?" Glasslight asked, when Marianne shivered as she recalled her time with the shadows, though she kept the details to herself. "Can't say I'm surprised. Their spell was a bit on the sinister side. Came across it in your neck of the woods, actually!"

Marianne, barely able to keep her eyes open at this point, only blinked, tired confusion plaguing her mind. "Hm?"

"Silver Edge! Only thing of use I've ever found there. Remember that one, Artie? Nasty grimoire."

Artie pulled at his coarse white beard. "Quite, quite. Leather binding. Lampblack ink. Point-four millimeter sheepskin parchment and a heavy iron clasp. Took four of my best workers to get that thing unhooked without damage, if I'm remembering correctly."

"Yes, you're always remembering correctly," Glasslight said flatly. "What *I* remember, is paying next to nothing for the thing! Must have been twenty years ago now. Your council seemed more than happy to be rid of it. Don't have to know the ins and outs of magic to feel the witch in those pages. Disagreeable old hag, if I've ever come across one."

"Part of the reason it took four workers! The first three refused to touch the book after it burned the tips of their fingers clean off. Right through their gloves, and everything! Glasslight had to wipe their poor memories. One bloke never could tackle his passion for beadwork again," Artie said.

He *tsk*ed sadly, while Marianne drank from her goblet of water, starting to wonder if she should rethink her interest in magic.

* * *

Marianne had barely shut her door when Emory's knock came later that night. To her surprise, in spite of her exhaustion, a small sense of anticipation fluttered through her stomach, followed by an unexpected swell of pleasure at the sight of Emory standing there, looking just as unkempt as she. A living reminder that, although he was her competition, neither were in it alone.

Emory swept his gaze over her and paused for a single breath before he pushed his way into the room, brushing past her as he did.

"Are you all right?" he said, once she had closed the door behind him.

"*Yes*," Marianne said, trying to muster a bit of indignation. But the word came out weaker than she would have preferred, undermining her point.

Emory, clearly unconvinced, surveyed her again, his eyes traveling over her slowly. Her face and neck heated, a thrill circling her throat when his gaze finally found hers.

"I . . ." he started, but his voice came out choked. He cleared his throat and tried again. "I could talk to him. Tell him it was too much."

At that, Marianne's indignation returned in full force. She would not be Emory's scapegoat. Yes, he had won all three rounds, but he hardly looked better than she.

"Don't you dare," Marianne said. "I'm fine. See? Nothing more than a stubbed toe. Somehow I think I'll survive."

"I didn't mean . . ." Emory huffed, running a hand through his dirty hair. "I didn't exactly have it easy out there. I just thought . . . I didn't mean anything by that. It's not that I don't think you can handle . . . whatever this is. But when you came out that last time, you looked . . ."

Marianne scoffed. That's *exactly* what Emory thought: that she couldn't handle it.

"At least I managed to keep my clothes in one piece," she said, nodding at the tattered remains of Emory's left sleeve and the bloodstains on his chest. "Did one of the shadows try to cut your heart out?"

A smile tugged at his mouth. "At least *I* didn't let a bird set about building its nest in my hair."

Marianne frowned, lifting a hand to her hair, but before she had a chance, Emory had closed the distance between them. Her breath caught, and she froze, her body still but her heart hammering as he slowly reached behind her, pulling a bent twig free from her braid.

He held it between them and Marianne reached up and took it, keeping her eyes on his all the while. She tried to parse his expression, but nothing could have prepared her for what he said next.

"I know what you're capable of, Marianne. And I want to beat you. Don't think I don't, and don't think I'll hold back. But . . . we're in this together. And . . ." he swallowed, his eyes moving to her lips as she let out an uneven breath. He watched her mouth a moment longer, leaning even closer. "And I'm clever enough to know my head start won't last. I *know* you. I know what you're capable of. Everyone else might underestimate you, Ree, but not me. Remember that."

* * *

As Marianne lay in bed that night, she forcefully willed away the feel of Emory's breath on her skin, the way his eyes had sharpened when he told her he knew what she was capable of. Instead, she thought about how to prove him right, how to make him work, how to *win*. Knowing he believed it to be a fair fight somehow made her want it more badly than ever. She could almost taste her longing on the back of her tongue, like the metallic taste of blood.

So she played her time in the forest over and over in her mind, trying to fit the pieces together, to reshape the paths she had taken in the dark, to make a plan. She could not—*would* not—have a repeat of today.

Pulling out her notebook, she wrote it all down.

* * *

The next day, Marianne won six times in a row.

Her first break came when she followed a hunch and learned that the glass baubles and their eerie ringing were actually a path guiding her to victory. Follow the sound, find the feather.

Of course, this was easier said than done, because along the path lay the most concentrated patches of enchanted earth. But during Marianne's brainstorming the previous evening, she had worked out that the ground softened in warning, and she was therefore able to avoid every greedy path of the jinxed earth.

As for the shadow stalkers, Marianne did have one unpleasant encounter. But using a jagged rock, she pried herself free—and then ran nearly face first into a puff of gold sparks. She managed to duck just in time before she stood, her chest heaving, as she stared at the beautiful glittering cloud.

Just then the tinkling of glass came again, and she rushed forward. But she wondered . . .

Running up to one of the trees housing hundreds of glass baubles, she reached up and plucked one free, studying it. It was something Glasslight had said at dinner when Emory complained of the dark.

"No need for darkness, dear boy. Take the light where you can find it!"

Sure enough, the glass bauble opened at the top. With a tiny gasp, Marianne hurried back to the sparkling cloud.

But there was no way to gather the gold flecks without submerging her hand, and she desperately wanted to avoid another round in the forest spent upside down.

So, hesitantly, slowly, she stretched the open bauble forward, inching the tips of her fingers as far back as possible while keeping a hold on the glass.

"Don't you dare try anything funny," she said sternly.

But a laugh escaped her lips when the gold sparks started to swirl and then move of their own accord into the small, delicate sphere. They spun faster and faster, continuing to spiral and eddy even once the last of the light crammed into the bauble and the top closed.

Using it to illuminate her path (and frighten away any wayward shadow stalkers), Marianne went on to find the feather in less than ten minutes.

* * *

"All right, all right, enough gloating. Just tell me your secret," Emory said with a laugh later that night.

He had come to her room again. Neither of them was nearly as spent as they had been after their first day in the forest, and he wanted to compare notes.

Marianne grinned, relishing his eagerness. She was seated on the sofa, her feet tucked under her and her hair wet from the bath she had taken, but Emory had collapsed on the rug. He looked up at her now, and maybe it was because she was viewing him upside down, but for the first time in years, it hit her exactly how handsome he was.

Finally, at the ridiculous frown he threw her way, she laughed and relented, kicking his shoulder playfully and explaining her strategy: the notes, the glass baubles, the warning signs for the enchanted earth.

"I did pick up on that one," he said. "But I actually spent all my time *looking* for those patches. I figured out in our second round, after falling through the fifth time, that they didn't drop you in a completely random spot in the forest. It was more like a maze. I started to map it out in my head and use it to help me get where I wanted to go."

"That's clever," Marianne said, impressed. It hadn't occurred to her. Even if it had, she was so anxious to be rid of the darkness, that the thought of trying to navigate it likely would have seemed too tedious. But it had gotten him three wins in a row.

Nothing, of course, compared to her six. Which she pointed out.

Emory grabbed one of the dozens of pillows she had shoved off her bed and threw it at her. "The next task is mine," he said, and something lighted beneath her skin.

She realized she couldn't wait to compete against him again. "Do you think that's what all of the tasks will be like?"

Emory sat up, his face thoughtful. "Glasslight strikes me as the sort of man who'll want to keep us on our toes. You remember I told you he hasn't taken an apprentice in more than twenty years? I think he'll be pulling out all the stops. Though I have to believe we'll do something a bit more practical. The description of an apprentice, after all, is to learn the trade of their mentor. I don't think Glasslight spends his days navigating magical forests."

Marianne nodded. She had figured as much, and there would likely come a time when they would begin shadowing his duties, rather than indulging Glasslight's desire to show off the magic he was forced to keep secret. That would mean meetings with the queen and foreign dignitaries, introductions for every noble man or woman across the kingdom, diplomatic strategy sessions, and more.

"Well, whatever he has in store, I guarantee you won't get the better of me again. I hope you enjoyed it while it lasted," Marianne said smugly. Then she threw the pillow back into Emory's face and laughed, her chest warming at his blinking, dazed expression.

12
THE LETTERS

THE NEXT TWO WEEKS WERE almost completely magic-free—and incredibly busy. Glasslight kept Marianne and Emory thoroughly engaged as he put the finishing touches on their second magical task. Mostly, this meant a staggering amount of paperwork. Marianne wasn't sure who had been in charge of such things before she and Emory arrived, but now Glasslight had a seemingly endless supply of tedious reports he insisted be sorted, copied, and summarized.

Sometimes, Artie would pop in, lending a quip or passing out chocolates before asking them to guess the mystery flavor (Marianne learned it was usually raspberry).

In addition, the two of them had been tasked with trailing Glasslight on his more mundane duties and writing up detailed observations of their findings for his memoir.

Most often, this meant watching him eat, handle the pettier petitions of the kingdom, and work on spellwork—which was especially tricky, considering Marianne and Emory were under spells of their own that prevented them from writing about such things.

As for Glasslight's more exciting undertakings—court sessions, diplomatic negotiations, meetings with the queen, and travel around the kingdom—Marianne and Emory were strictly excluded. Those responsibilities were for the official apprentice only, once he or she secured their place at the end of summer.

Glasslight was off at some such meeting now, which gave Marianne the first opportunity in days to take a moment to herself. She sat at the desk in her room and pulled out the small pile of letters she had amassed in the past week, hoping it would ease the niggle of guilt she felt at keeping Ilya waiting so long between correspondence.

Aside from a short congratulatory letter from the village elder's office in Silver Edge, an elaborately addressed envelope without a return label, and an abrasive note from Ilya's best friend, Angelica Martin, demanding Marianne "wipe the floor with that Leroux boy," there was only Ilya's most recent letter.

Marianne slid the dagger-shaped opener beneath the wax seal and smiled her way through the contents, laughing at some of her mother's reports of recent commissions and goings on.

Angelica has requested another sweater for her dog, Marianne read, nearing the end of Ilya's letter. *This time I suggested orange and white* stripes *instead of polka dots.*

Marianne smiled. Angelica Martin had no fewer than twelve sweaters, all in shades of orange and white, for her small, shaggy dog. Aside from being Ilya's best friend, she was also one of her most loyal customers, if one counted objects purchased. (Unfortunately, considering Ilya usually traded her work with Angelica for various seeds to plant in their garden, she wasn't exactly one of her most lucrative clients.)

Ilya's letter went on to detail a few of her more interesting commissions made by letter-request from people across the kingdom, and expressing her relief that Marianne had reached Queensmont with no casualties other than a minor irritation at her travel companion's continual post-dinner visits at the inns along the way.

She ended with a simple: *Hang in there, sweet. The answers will come.*

Marianne paused at this. Her initial letter to Ilya had been mostly full of complaints about Emory. It was strange to think how much had already changed. Not that Marianne didn't still find his constant cheerfulness and intrusions irritating, but she did find herself allowing some of their previous childhood familiarity to seep back in. And it wouldn't change the fact that she still fully intended to beat him. Make a clean sweep of all three tasks.

Just to prove she could.

Putting Ilya's letter away, Marianne turned over the unmarked one in her stack, her fingers stilling as she read the return address situated on the back.

Jasper Leroux.

Marianne stared, her eyes roving over the ink strokes again, convinced she had somehow misread. But they stayed firmly fixed in place. Jasper Leroux. Care of Silver Edge.

For a moment, she considered not opening it. But her curiosity eventually got the best of her. Tearing open the wax seal, she unfolded the small paper, her eyes scanning the tight, elaborate script.

Dear Miss Finch,

I sincerely hope this letter finds you well. I've heard from Emory and you should know he offers nothing but glowing reviews for both you and the extraordinarily hard work you've put in so far this summer. Master Glasslight, as well, only receives my son's finest compliments.

My fatherly tendencies, however, cannot be so easily stifled. I remember you from when you were a girl, Miss Finch. Always happy to speak your mind, just like your mother, and so I hoped I might be able to appeal to your sense of candor.

You see, I fear my son is only willing to pass along the rosier aspects of your education. But perhaps you might be persuaded to speak a little more freely? I wonder, how is Master Glasslight treating you? What sort of experiences is he offering? How exactly is he deciding the victor for this little contest he's pulled the two of you into?

I'm afraid I got the distinct sense that my son was holding back, and I wouldn't want you to get hurt. I hope you know you have a friendly face to reach out to should you find yourself in over your head.

I don't want to alarm you, of course, but the scenario is a bit questionable, to say the least. I fear your mother may not have recognized that—through no fault of her own, I assure you, these concerns are merely something born from a certain class of experience—and so she may not have prepared you properly. It is my duty, however, to protect my son, as well as you. Unlike Emory and the two years he spent in travel, I fear your youth hasn't trained you for the world quite yet.

I would be remiss if I didn't do my own due diligence. I wouldn't want you to struggle needlessly. And your forthrightness about Master Glasslight will be of remarkable help as I continue to sort out the situation.

Please don't think me too abrasive. My son's trust in you has bred my own faith that we are indeed on the same team, Miss Finch.

Hoping to hear from you soon,

Jasper Leroux

Marianne finished reading with a scowl, just barely preventing herself from crumpling the letter and tossing it in the fire. Instead, she put it aside, wishing she could so easily cast off the taste it had left in her mouth, the words imprinted on the backs of her eyes in Jasper's flourished, deliberate hand. *Little contest . . . in over your head . . . your youth hasn't prepared you.* She could almost hear his oily voice, see the sneer on his face.

Still, she deliberately slowed her frustrated, shallow breathing for a second, forcing herself, just for the sake of being comprehensive, to consider:

Was there a possibility he was right? Yes, Jasper Leroux was arrogant and biased, but buried beneath that, could he see something about Marianne and her inexperience that she couldn't?

No. The answer came swift and sure.

The truth was, in spite of her growing ease with Emory, Marianne did not trust Jasper Leroux.

It wasn't just the oil that seemed to coat her insides at the mere mention of his name. After their departure from Silver Edge, she couldn't help picturing the way Emory also shifted when in his presence. A flatter edge to his expressions. A dulling of his infectious enthusiasm. A more careful tilt to his posture. A different version of himself, designed to please his father.

Had it always been there? As children, Emory took any opportunity he could to avoid his house, so Marianne saw the two of them together very rarely. Instead, they'd spend their days in the woods or Ilya's workshop.

But even then, Marianne knew that Jasper wanted only one thing: For Emory to win. At everything.

In an effort to distract herself, she started work on her next letter to her mother, trying to quell the prickle of distaste in her throat.

While the spell Glasslight had her and Emory under didn't allow Marianne to speak of the magic, she was able to give some impressions of the palace and the bustling city of Queensmont they had passed through, which lifted her spirits a surprising amount.

She also couldn't help but describe, in pleasant detail, Glasslight's cheerful attitudes that could quickly devolve into thunderous mood swings (especially when in the presence of Artie, who seemed to enjoy riling him up), and Emory's continual insistence that he would come out ahead at the end of the apprenticeship, only stoking Marianne's desire to win.

Before long, she had managed to lose herself fully in her descriptions, Jasper and his letter fading to nothing more than a lingering shadow at the back of her mind.

13

THE MIRRORED HALL

"WOULD YOU TWO CUT THAT out?" Glasslight chided.

Emory turned his head toward the booming voice just as Marianne slashed her arm through the air. "Wha—ow!"

Clapping a hand to her mouth, Marianne stifled a laugh. She supposed their game of swordplay involving fallen tree branches in the courtyard had been bound to take a turn at some point. And a sharp knock to the side of Emory's head was definitely a turn.

Glasslight shook his head in exasperation as he continued striding toward them. "I'm surrounded by mediocrity. Do neither of you care that today is the first day of the rest of your lives?"

"Didn't you say that yesterday?" Marianne asked, leaning on Emory's shoulder as he vigorously rubbed his temple, wincing in pain.

"So what if I did? I was right!"

"Apologies, Master Glasslight. We didn't hear you coming," Emory said, still holding a hand to his head. At least there didn't seem to be any blood.

"You should always expect me! You should always expect anything! Have you learned nothing in our time together?"

"'Expect the unexpected,'" Marianne offered, quoting Glasslight's note from the first night she arrived at the palace.

"Yes. Thank you, Miss Finch," Glasslight said, placated for the time being. "Glad to hear someone has been paying attention."

She flashed a smug smile at Emory.

Glasslight examined his nails. "Anyway, not that either of you seem to care, but today happens to be your second task."

Marianne and Emory snapped into attention, their full focus now on Glasslight.

"What?" Marianne said.

"When?" Emory asked.

"Where?"

"Oh, now I have your attention. Well, good. Then I expect to see you at seven o'clock in Gelder Hall. Do not be late. And dress accordingly."

Marianne glanced down at her skirts. "According to what?"

But Glasslight was already pacing away. He waved a single hand over his shoulder in farewell, shouting, "Seven o'clock!"

* * *

At six forty-five sharp, the knock came at Marianne's door.

She opened it and pretended to narrow her eyes in suspicion at the sight of Emory at the threshold.

"Tell the truth," she said. "Are you, or are you not, here to weaken my defenses?"

Emory grinned. "I don't need to resort to low-handed tactics in order to win, Ree."

She laughed and moved into the hall, shutting the door behind her, moving in step with Emory, arm in arm as she grasped his elbow.

The hallways were wide, with tall ivory-painted arches and patterned wallpapers, and yet the two of them walked close together.

In preparation for their second of the three magical tasks, Glasslight was waiting for them in what seemed to be a remote part of the palace. Led by a guard, they passed bustling servants and animated members of the court on their way. Emory doled out his usual greetings. It seemed that since their initial arrival, he had made the acquaintance of several more palace individuals—both court members and servants alike.

A woman carrying a bundle of dresses squeezed past, reminding Marianne of her mother. When Marianne tried to smile, the woman cast her eyes down.

They should know their places.

Jasper Leroux's words rose into Marianne's mind. She suddenly became hyper-aware of Emory walking in step with her, the feel of his arm beneath her fingers. Had he realized how wrong his father was? Or did he still agree? Did he still bite out his snide remarks when Marianne wasn't around to hear?

She blinked, aware she was breathing a little too fast, and dropped Emory's arm. His brow creased in concern as he peered over at her, and she wondered if he could sense the shift in her stance. Afraid of how easily he might read her, she refused to meet his eyes.

When they finally reached Glasslight, he was standing between two closed doors. The sight of him pushed Marianne's unwelcome musings from her mind, bringing her back to the present. She loosened her fists, making space in her chest for a renewed sense of determination.

Because Emory wasn't her enemy—he was her competition.

For once, Marianne was pleased to note, Tiago was resting happily at Glasslight's feet, rather than fruitlessly trailing his nonstop movement. Next to them, however, Artie couldn't seem to stand still. He was bouncing, his expression positively gleeful.

"Party Artie!" Emory said, squeezing the tiny man's narrow shoulder. "If you're here then we know the fun can begin."

"Hello Emory!" Artie responded, then, greeting her the same way he had every time he'd seen her for the past two weeks, "And my Marianne."

Marianne grinned.

Over their time together, Emory had become "everyone's favorite Emory," due, according to Artie, to his natural charm and enthusiasm, and the way it infected everyone Emory came into contact with, bringing a smile to their faces, making them feel seen and important.

It was a trait Marianne was admiring more with each passing day and each new face. The way, unlike her, that Emory never tired, was always exuberant. Always genuinely pleased to make a new acquaintance or reunite with an old one. Always able to offer his full self and somehow make it feel like a precious gift.

Artie had noticed this early on, and had shortly afterward taken to walking into a room with the two of them and saying, "Well, if it isn't everyone's favorite Emory!"

But then he'd turn to Marianne and add, "And my own Marianne. The secretly ooey-gooey ice queen of my heart." Then he would wink, and she would smile, another chip of the ice she couldn't hide from him thawing away.

"Real magic!" Artie squeaked now, his bushy white beard quivering with the movement. "I tell you, it never gets old! Not even after seventy years!"

"Perhaps that's because I made you forget after your attitude at the end of the last task," Glasslight noted. "I hope it taught you a little something."

Artie waved this comment away. "We both know the memories came rushing back when that wrinkled face of yours entered my sight. I say, there are easier ways to get friends, man. No need to bribe them with promises of the supernatural! Not that it doesn't work quite swimmingly," he added to Marianne, who was busy suppressing a laugh.

Glasslight's mouth hung open. "*Wrinkled*? When was the last time you looked in a mirror, old man? I ought to take it all away for good! And I'll have you know there's an entire *kingdom* eager to partake in both my sparkling personality and unparalleled intellect. And that's even with most of my formidable talent hidden under a bushel for everyone in the kingdom except you three lousy, ungrateful —"

"Master Glasslight?" Emory interrupted, his tone polite. "May I ask what our task is today?"

"What? Oh, yes, well . . ." Glasslight trailed off, his face leaching some of its splotchy red as he refocused on the reason they were all gathered.

"Today's task is about several things. Honesty, integrity, vulnerability—but mostly it's about knowing oneself. It was only once I embraced the magnificent man I am that I was able to truly step into my potential, and the same will be true for you. Or, ah . . . you," he said, trailing his gaze from Marianne to Emory. "You can't expect to communicate with others if you can't communicate with yourself! Trust me. Sixty-six years I've served as royal advisor."

"Ooh, tell them what they're going to do. Go on, tell them," Artie said, his creaking voice trembling with anticipation.

Glasslight, who seemed to have forgotten his indignation, grinned in a self-satisfied way. "Particularly brilliant bit of magic, if you ask me. Not that anyone's around to truly appreciate it. I tell you, being the only wizard in the world has its drawbacks. But your ignorant admiration will have to do.

"The premise is simple. You will each enter through one of the doors behind me. Once inside, you will find a chamber filled with . . . truth. Or lies. Your job is to discern what is what. Simply touch the pieces of yourself that are true, and ignore the rest. Whoever has collected the most truths before your time runs out, wins."

Glasslight smiled, clearly pleased with his speech. His silvery beard had been curled into ringlets today, and for the first time, it was untucked, reaching nearly to his knees.

"You forgot the most important part!" Artie squeaked.

Rolling his eyes, Glasslight adjusted the sleeve of his shirt and said flatly, "And Artie here will be your timekeeper."

Artie beamed as he displayed an elaborate gold hourglass from behind his back. "Ready?" he said, his eyes bright.

Marianne looked instinctively at Emory. He was already watching her, a smile on his face, though it wasn't as broad as usual. He was too busy studying her, a question in his eyes.

She smiled, and his face softened, reassured. Her body gave an unexpected ache in response.

"Go!"

Marianne and Emory hesitated, turning back to Glasslight in unison. "How long—" Emory asked, just as she started to say, "Does it matter which door—"

But Glasslight used his enormous hands to push each of them through separately. Before she knew it, the hallway behind her was cut off and she was entirely alone.

For a moment, everything around her was dim, and then a thousand candles soared to life. At *least* a thousand. Maybe ten thousand. They glittered and flickered and . . .

Marianne squinted. No. There weren't ten thousand candles, there were ten thousand *reflections*. Not that there weren't plenty of candles—in the crystal chandelier, lining gaps on the walls, floating in the air around Marianne. She spun in a circle, any thoughts of a timer or the task at hand completely forgotten for a moment as her breath stalled in her chest.

It was beautiful.

Every part of her wanted to know *how*, wished she could pick apart the magic and understand all of its disparate parts, but then the hiss of sand through an hourglass somehow slid down the back of her neck and Marianne's focus promptly snapped back. She stopped spinning, trying to remember what Glasslight had said.

Truth. He wanted her to find truth. An infuriatingly vague notion, but she was certain that if she could just focus, she'd have as little trouble conquering this task as she had the forest.

Well. Hopefully less.

In the forest, a frazzled, surprised mind had led to frazzled, weak results. Today, Marianne would stay calm. She would use logic.

Moving closer to the walls, nervously rocking her head side to side, she peered into one of what she realized were dozens and dozens of mirrors.

Some were too high even for her to reach, some nearly touched the floor from their spot on the wall. As she stared at herself staring back at her, her dark hair plaited and falling over her shoulder, her green eyes muddled with confusion and impatience—with *hunger*—the mirror started to change.

They all did.

Suddenly the thousands of pinpricks of candlelight were wiped from the smooth surfaces of the mirrors, and . . . *moments* started to play out.

It was like watching through a window, except in each of the frames, there was Marianne.

She watched herself helping her mother in her workshop.

And there she was buying buns from her favorite pastry cart in Silver Edge.

Marianne putting her feet in the stream at home, and having tea with her mother and Angelica Martin, the three of them laughing while Angelica's dog howled at passersby through the open window.

Truth. That's what Glasslight had said. She needed to claim these pieces of herself that belonged to her. Marianne reached out a hesitant hand, then stopped. How did one claim a living daydream of oneself? These images rang true, but they weren't *memories*. The colors were slightly off, the details unwilling to fit into specific times or places. But they were still hers.

The things Marianne loved. The things she wanted.

Unsure what else to do, she touched the frame around herself, Ilya, and Angelica Martin.

It heated, and Marianne flinched away, watching in nervous anticipation as a strange sound filled the spacious room, bouncing off the polished wood floors and glass surfaces of the mirrors. It was like a soft ringing of metal, as though a coin were bouncing around in a tin pitcher, growing steadily louder.

Suddenly, a gap opened at the bottom of the frame. The sound increased in volume and Marianne stretched forward, curious, anxious—

Something small and round zoomed out of the opening. Marianne ducked, throwing her arms over her head. But nothing hit her or the ground around her. She looked up to find a small marble hovering in the air in front of her.

"Well, hello there," she said, blinking at it with fascination. It was made of a lustrous material that glinted in the light of the candles, almost like a pearl, but when she reached out to touch it with her fingertips, Marianne found herself unable to grasp it. There was . . . something there, more than just air.

"What *are* you?" She pushed against it, making the marble orbit around her, though it seemed reluctant to stray more than a few inches away . . .

Remembering she was working against a clock, Marianne tore her gaze from the tiny pearlescent orb. How much more time did she have? Neither Master Winthrop nor Master Glasslight had said.

Forcing herself to focus, Marianne moved her gaze up.

A strange emotion pooled in her stomach as her eyes landed on the mirror directly above the frame from which the marble had emerged. She couldn't quite place the feeling. Embarrassment? For a moment, she thought it might be a strange sort of glee . . . But no, it couldn't be that. Marianne would never delight in the moment playing out before her . . .

In it, Marianne was sneaking into Mrs. Pettlewhip's bedroom while she slept. Silvery moonlight colored the small bed. Tiptoeing, Marianne wound to Mrs. Pettlewhip's side and reached out her hand. There was something in her grip, something that glinted even through the darkness . . . a pair of scissors. Marianne watched pure determination and satisfaction color her face as the tiny version of herself reached out and clipped Mrs. Pettlewhip's hair, once, twice, three times. She leaned back, surveying her work—

Marianne pivoted on her feet to look away. That was absolutely, unequivocally *not* truth. She might despise Mrs. Pettlewhip and the hateful lies and gossip the woman represented, but Marianne would never stoop to anything so petty.

Unfortunately, it only grew worse from there.

The next moving moment Marianne focused on showed her obviously being praised. Glasslight stood in front of her, tall and buoyant, squeezing Marianne's shoulder with his gigantic hand, his mouth moving in silent words, his face glowing with pride—

No. Marianne didn't care about that. She wanted to beat Emory, but not because she craved Glasslight's praise. Nor did she need to meet the queen, who was the subject of the next moment. The two of them were laughing, the queen's crown balanced regally on her head. Marianne recognized their monarch from the painted sketches in one of her books.

She also didn't need the rapt attention of Silver Edge as she presented something in front of the village council. Nor to travel to an ocean and stand at the edge of it, the wind whipping her blouse.

She didn't need to wander the busy streets of Queensmont.

She didn't need her own home, filled with books; she was happy with her mother.

She certainly didn't need any moment involving her holding a long, silver dagger, her eyes blazing and her hair chaotic as she stared at something out of frame, her chest heaving.

She didn't need . . . Marianne swallowed as she watched a tiny version of herself march up to an elaborate door set in a three-story manor, the name PELROY stamped across the gate as she passed it.

No . . . no. Marianne didn't need to find her father, wherever he was, or to confront him.

But when Marianne turned away from that particular mirror, she felt as though the floor dropped from beneath her feet. She was falling, the room too bright, too colorful, too unsteady as her gaze narrowed in on an assortment of mirrors. Marianne shouting at Emory . . . no, at his father, no at Emory . . . The figure in front of her shifted, but her features never wavered from their fierce, angry determination as she silently raged.

And then her face flushed as her eyes found an image of her being embraced by Emory as she cried . . . Another one of her being held by him, crushed by him, as he kissed her . . .

Marianne's mouth went slack, her cheeks blazing, even though there was no one else around to see the image. For the first time, she wondered where they had come from. *How* had Glasslight created these?

A rushing filled her ears, like bags and bags of sand through an enormous hourglass. The sound slithered down her back as if it had structure and form, and she quickly realized it was coming from the room itself.

She guessed her time was running out. Whipping her head around in a frenzy, she touched the image of herself in her mother's workshop and the one of her purchasing a bun from the cart down the street.

After taking one more circle, she spotted one of her with what looked to be the components of a grain thresher scattered around her as she examined the parts, tapping her chin with a pencil, her notebook splayed in front of her.

She touched it for good measure, listening to the metal clanging as another pearl shot from the slot that opened at the bottom of the frame. It had just fallen into her orbit, levitating somewhere near her elbow, when all the candles extinguished and the door behind her reopened.

Glasslight appeared there, beaming. He took one look at her, however, and something in his expression shifted, a cloud of disappointment passing over his face as he waved her forward.

Marianne's stomach clenched. What had she done wrong? But the answer became clear the moment she rejoined Glasslight in the hallway. Standing there, in conversation with Artie, was Emory—with *dozens* of pearlescent marbles floating around him.

Marianne's embarrassment turned sticky and hot, coating her throat and dripping slowly into her stomach as she stared at the four orbs she had collected.

"Marianne," Glasslight said gently, walking over to her, Tiago springing into excruciatingly slow action as the porcelain tortoise attempted to follow. "What happened?"

Marianne tried to clear the lump of embarrassment from her throat. She could see Emory and Artie turn their attention toward her, and she wished she could flee. "What do you mean?"

"There were well over a hundred pieces in there, my girl. And this is what you come out with?"

"You . . . you said to search for truth," she answered, forcing her voice to become stronger, to ground her, even as her body felt as if it was made of smoke, unable to hold her in place. "I gathered the pieces of myself that were true. I completed the task."

She forced herself not to glance at Emory, who had gone very still. Even without turning her head, she could tell Artie had stopped his normal bouncing.

Glasslight was silent for a long time. He twisted a silvery ringlet from his beard between his thumb and forefinger, his dark violet eyes inspecting Marianne's face. "Perhaps you'd like to take another look. Perhaps you can . . . quiet your mind this time. Pay closer attention to how you *feel*. Your heart. It's important to let the truths ring *inside* of you."

Marianne blinked, the words ricocheting with painful pricks against her ribs and muscles, like thrown needles. In an instant, she was suddenly standing in front of her mother's tapestries again, staring at the dullness that had come over her face, the staleness in her captured movement. *I'm afraid, somewhere along the way, you forgot how to know your heart.*

But maybe . . . maybe it didn't even matter. Because in terms of truth, there was only a single one staring Marianne in the face as she stood there in that hall:

She had failed. Again.

Maybe Jasper had been right. Maybe she never really had a chance at all. Marianne had burst into the *palace* and let her blind ignorance—her arrogance—trick her into thinking she had a chance, despite her inexperience and naivety. She had deluded herself into thinking whether she won or lost could be her choice, that she could prove herself somehow. And for what?

For nothing more, in the end, than pride. A dazzling opportunity Marianne secretly, selfishly longed for.

In the end, she had done nothing more than step out of the shadows and proved to everyone that she was exactly what they thought.

"No," Marianne said, a bit too loudly. "I don't want to go back. If . . . if you want to take another look"—her fingers started to tremble, and so she clenched her fists, forcing the next words out —"maybe you'll see it was *you* who made the mistake, not me."

Glasslight's face darkened. After a long pause, he said simply, "Mistake?"

Her humiliation swelled, making the moment unbearable. So she set her jaw and took a breath and pressed it into something more useful: anger.

"Yes. What right do you have to try and . . . sway me? It's one thing to guide or impart your hard-earned wisdom; it's another to try and . . . and *mold* me to what you believe your protégé *should* be. Those images in there were not me, and I will not fall for your tricks. You plant your seed of doubt in my mind and send me in again until I fold to your will? Your idea of who I should be?"

Marianne's voice was loud enough that it echoed around the hall, drawing even more attention to herself and her foolishness as she single-handedly ruined everything. Ilya's business had barely survived a baseless rumor—what would happen if the world learned Marianne had shouted and raged at one of the most respected men in the kingdom? Had been thrown out and condemned by the palace itself?

Because that was what she was asking for with every blow. Her wrath in this moment had the power to crumble their lives. To wipe away their future. But still, she couldn't stop the words, even as Glasslight's face contorted with fury.

"I am not a puppet on a string. I am not a dancing bear!" she finished, now shouting, horrified by her choice of words.

She wouldn't allow herself to look at Emory. Instead, she drew herself up as high as she could, though it didn't change the fact that she still had to tilt her head back to look into Glasslight's eyes as they popped with rage.

He spluttered, momentarily overcome. "Girl, you have no *idea*. No idea! How *dare* you! Shame on me for thinking you *could* be guided, for thinking you had a few brains!"

"Master Glasslight," Emory said, stepping forward, the tiny spheres of luminescent pearls around him swirling faster, disturbed by his sudden movement. His voice was hard, his eyes blazing.

"This doesn't concern you, boy."

"It does when I'm forced to stand here and listen to someone who is supposed to be a wise mentor spewing stupidity."

The room stilled. Artie, whistling low, made a show of taking a step back. But Marianne's chest caved in as she spun her gaze to Emory. What was he *doing*?

"*Stupidi*—" Glasslight started.

"Sir, with all due respect, you have no idea what you're talking about. You have no idea what you've stumbled into with Marianne. How lucky you are."

"Luck? LUCK!" Glasslight thundered. "I'm surrounded by insolence! INCOMPETENCE!"

Marianne opened and closed her mouth, all of her words dried up. She watched Emory, her heart racing, as he continued to stare at Glasslight. She didn't—couldn't—fully trust his words, and yet . . . she wanted to. They softened the sharp edges of her outrage and fear, blurring it into utter bewilderment.

This was the very boy who had stoked all of her wildest insecurities, her fiercest anger. Six years ago he had broken her heart. After that, Marianne had hidden; had confined her world to what was safe. And now he was standing here risking his future to defend her. She didn't understand him at all.

She didn't understand anything.

"Oh dear . . ." Artie said, clicking his tongue, the sound grating against Marianne's skin as it brought her attention back. *Tsk, tsk, tsk.*

Not knowing what else to do—what else she could do—Marianne cast one last look at Emory and Glasslight before turning on her heel and fleeing.

"Now, just wait one second! You're covered in *magic!*" Glasslight called after her, but she didn't look back. She barely registered the tiny pearls circling her torso until she heard a clap, followed by a strange, hissed word, and saw them wink out of existence.

14

THE ROSE GARDEN

GLASSLIGHT HADN'T EXACTLY FORBIDDEN THEM from exploring the palace, but after spending nearly three weeks being escorted by guards through its halls, Marianne was fairly certain it was implied that they weren't meant to wander off on their own.

And yet, no one had rushed after her. So she told herself it was fine as she twisted through the hallways, earning more than one bewildered stare at her hurried feet and stone-faced expression.

Finally, she located a door that led outside. Bursting through it, she found herself in a small, walled-in courtyard. The sun was setting, bleeding the last of its glazed gold over the ivied wall in front of her.

Blessedly, the space was empty, filled only with hedges and potted plants, and the smell of jasmine and honeysuckle. The scents mingled through the air, settling Marianne's shoulders. She thought of her mother's teas and the garden between their workshop and home. There was a small arched gateway at the far end of the courtyard that led to an enclosed path, a burst of roses in all different colors climbing over one another at its edges.

Marianne headed for it, willing her mind to untangle while also forcing herself not to think of the gravity of what she had just done—the inevitable fallout she would face. She wended her way into the rose garden through the twisting path until she could no longer see the courtyard beyond it. Roses of every color crowded the space: yellows, pinks, purples, whites. Some were larger than her fist, while others had barely started to bud. Marianne breathed in their light scent, letting it wipe away all thought until the sound of footsteps made her turn.

She stilled when Emory came into view. "Did you follow me?"

The tiny pearls were no longer suspended around him. For the first time, Marianne felt a stab of guilt for having run off so recklessly, risking exposure of Glasslight's magic to the entire palace in her rage.

"I asked if anyone had seen you," Emory answered, pausing his steps, prompting Marianne to finally look up. When she did, the expression on his face gave her a renewed swoop of unease. She couldn't decipher it at all. It was . . . detached. And oddly formal. With a rush of cold, she realized the flicker of disappointment she sometimes noted in his eyes had crowded his entire face.

When he didn't speak again she said, uncertainly, not even sure whether or not she meant it, "I don't need your concern."

The truth was, his words to Glasslight had felt good, like a burden lifted. A hint that she might not have to carry everything herself. But then—

"Good, because you don't have it," Emory said, a strange bite to his words. They zapped her skin like the tiny electric shocks.

"Well . . . good? Emory—"

"Marianne, what was that?"

"What was what?" she asked, confused.

"You . . ." He trailed off, dropping onto a bench as some of his peculiar formality fell away. "You can't just run away or lash out when things get hard. You're better than that, Marianne. We're in this together, remember?"

"Emory, believe it or not, this has nothing to do with you," Marianne said irritably. "We're supposed to be here to *learn*. Whatever Glasslight was doing back there was not that. You should be angry with *him*."

"He shouldn't have spoken to you like that, but . . . Marianne, he *was* teaching us. Why are you so unwilling to see that? I don't get it. You used to love to learn. You weren't so afraid to be pushed—you welcomed it. What happened?"

Marianne stayed silent, listening to the hum of bees, her pulse fluttering as she watched Emory look up at her with a flicker of sadness. She wanted to take it away but she didn't know how. She didn't understand what she did to make him feel that way, and if she answered his question, it would only bring more sorrow into those eyes.

"I always admired you. Did you know that?" he went on, his gaze fastened on her, holding her in place. "You were so sure of yourself. You wanted to know everything, and I genuinely believed you *did*, even when you were ten years old." He smiled. "Even though you were younger and smart-mouthed and always lost in your own world, because of you, I wanted to try harder. To be better. To be *more*.

"My father . . . he made me feel like I was only capable of what he said I could do. And even then, only with his constant supervision and nitpicking, so I tried to please him. I . . . I still do. And it always felt awful because I knew it was never enough. But when I watched you, it was the first time it ever occurred to me that I could want things for myself. It was the first time it occurred to me I could make decisions on my own. And I did. Even when you shut me out, I thought of you so often. I pictured your hand shooting into the air to challenge the tutor or those notes you were always writing. You showed me a drawing you had made of the watermill once. Do you remember that? You had drawn out all of the pieces, with arrows and diagrams showing where they went and how they worked together. I was eleven, and I remember feeling like my world had just shifted. It became somehow bigger and more focused all at once. There was you, and I only wanted to see you, but you saw . . . everything else. I never once thought to question how the watermill—or anything—worked. I didn't care. But watching you—seeing the world through your eyes—opened up everything for me."

He paused. Marianne's chest was moving up and down —she could feel it—so why did she have the sense that she couldn't breathe?

When Emory spoke again, it came out as a whisper. "And then you disappeared. You stopped talking to me, and I didn't understand why. My world became smaller when you walked out of it, Marianne. I traveled the entire kingdom for two years and none of it felt as grand or important as watching your mind at work. Nothing was as thrilling as trying to keep up with you."

Marianne's mind was nothing but white noise. She watched, frozen, her heart thrumming as Emory slowly stood and moved closer to her.

Was that really how he saw her? She had *heard* him. *Dim-witted dolts*, Jasper had said. And Emory agreed. He *agreed*. She could still hear his voice behind that door.

Every one of them.

But she could see now it wasn't just her who had felt the loss of their friendship. The hurt was etched on his face. And for a moment, Marianne wanted—*longed*—to see herself the way he did. To reclaim what she once had. With Emory and with her own mind. Her own heart.

She moved closer to him, suddenly yearning for his touch, his belief in her. As she reached out and cautiously put a hand to his chest, Marianne realized she was desperate for Emory in a different way than she ever had been. She was *craving* him. Enough to make her head spin.

Emory swallowed. She watched his throat move and his eyes fall to her mouth, and her skin shivered. Everything seemed to dance across the surface of her neck and shoulders: the light wavering as a breeze moved the tallest roses back and forth, creating a ripple of shadows; the scent of the flowers; and Emory. Emory seemed to be clouding all her senses. Their touch was narrowed to the surface of her palm against his chest, and yet she felt him everywhere.

When he spoke again, she could feel his breath on her nose and cheekbones as he bent closer to her.

"Please don't lock me out again, Marianne. I don't know what I did before, or how to stop it from happening again. You're my best friend. You always have been. I feel so helpless. I'm trying so hard but I don't feel like it's making a difference. Just tell me what to do."

She watched her hand splay across the soft linen of his shirt and resisted the urge to claw her fingers closed and crumple the fabric tightly as she pulled him closer.

Instead, she closed her eyes, lifting onto her toes as he bent his head. His hand reached out and ran tenderly along the length of her braid. She felt upended, as if she were back in the forest, dizzily watching the world turn on its head.

"I don't know what you saw in there," Emory whispered slowly, pausing a moment, cautiously trying to catch her eye.

She wanted to reach up and wind her arms around his neck. To press her mouth against his—to feel him and taste him, but also to keep him from speaking so that she didn't have to hear. So that she could preserve this moment.

But she didn't. And he went on.

"I may not know, but . . . it was you, Marianne. All of it. I . . ."—a breath out through his nose—"I asked. Glasslight said the spell was his. He called it fate. He said it projected pieces of whoever was inside the room onto the mirrors. The truth was everywhere."

A single beat passed, bringing the world back into focus, and then Marianne's heels dropped onto the stone path. She didn't want to hear anymore. She didn't want to think about any of it. The apprenticeship. The magic. The visions and the tasks. She couldn't. Not when she had ruined it.

She let her hand fall from his chest and took a step back. "It doesn't matter," she said. "I'm not here for any of that, Emory. I may have wanted those pieces of me once. But . . . not anymore."

He shook his head. "I don't believe you."

She stared at him for a long time, searching for her voice. She couldn't give him what he wanted. She couldn't be what he thought she was. Especially because Marianne wasn't sure anymore what version of herself he held in his mind. Was she a dancing bear or Emory's window to the world? Some untouchable ideal she could never live up to?

Both were untrue. Both hurt.

"I'm sorry . . . I'm sorry I cut you out without explaining why. But it's not about us anymore, Emory. I didn't . . . understand. When I was a child. I didn't understand how hard my mother worked while I ran around in my own worlds, stealing away for hours every day at your manor to learn things I'd never need. I was selfish."

It was a partial truth, at least.

His brow was furrowed as he began to say, "Marianne —"

"Emory, I'm tired. And I need to pack. I should go home before facing the humiliation of Glasslight telling me to do so himself."

She took another step back from Emory, putting as much distance as possible between them on the narrow path. He shook his head, opening his mouth to speak. She turned on her heel and walked away before he could try and stop her.

15

THE TEA

THE TRAY WAS BEAUTIFUL.

Marianne wasn't sure what had motivated her to ask for it, except that if she was going to leave the palace, she wanted to partake in this one last thing. For her mother. She wouldn't be bringing home anything of real use, but she could offer this.

That's why she stood next to the velvet sofa in her room, staring down at the sterling silver tray on the small table in front of it. It was laid out with the most intricate porcelain tea set she had ever seen. It almost reminded her of Tiago, and she was struck by how outrageous it all was.

A wizard. A vision. A set of magical trials to earn a fated apprenticeship. A tortoise made of porcelain.

And Marianne realized how desperately she would miss it.

But there was no reason for such sentiment. She had only known Glasslight, Artie, and Tiago for a few weeks. And Emory had been gone from her life for six years. She would go back to the way things were. The way she had always planned.

Next to the tea set were several sprigs of herbs. Marianne had asked for an assortment. She wanted to see what sort of ingredients the palace had at its disposal. She recognized most of the tied bundles on the tray—rosemary, lavender, rosehips. But there were a couple of unfamiliar mushrooms and herbs. Whoever had arranged the tray took the time to label them, and Marianne couldn't help but smile in admiration at the meticulous handwriting and added description—

There was a sprig of green with delicate white petals (*stitchwort—for pain*); a bundle of tall, narrow mushrooms (*oakcaps—for nausea*); a pile of tiny bluish seeds, so small Marianne might have missed them if not for the label and their bright, tangy scent (*vress—for sleep; small doses only*); and more, all organized and clearly identified, with descriptions just as lovely to Marianne as the arrangement itself.

She wanted to make notes of them in her notebook. To sketch out each ingredient and look through her books to see if there was anything she could add.

Marianne didn't have the same love for botany as she did for her other pursuits—engineering, history, politics, art—but she could appreciate thoroughness in any capacity. And at least this could be of use when she arrived back in Silver Edge.

After staring at the tray for several long minutes, however, she let out a sigh and carefully packed most of the ingredients away to bring to her mother. Ilya wouldn't have heard of the ingredients either, but she and Angelica Martin would admire their uniqueness and extravagance, tied and bound so beautifully.

Once they were put away, Marianne reached for a few of the laid-out ingredients, then stripped and bagged a familiar pine needle and juniper berry blend her mother often made. She breathed in the tart, woody scent, adding in a few extra ingredients at the last minute. It was seeping in the teapot when someone knocked at her door.

Marianne straightened. She wasn't ready to face Emory again. Her chest was a jumble of confusion and longing and disappointment and anger. She couldn't sort it out, and she wasn't sure what sort of frenzy it might create in her when she saw his face.

But when Marianne opened her door, it wasn't Emory standing there.

"Artie?"

"My Marianne!" he squeaked, and despite everything, Marianne couldn't stop the smile that lifted the corner of her lips. It was the mere sight of Artie, barely reaching her chin from where he stooped, with his bushy white beard and his crinkled eyes and his bouncing toes and the way he beamed as she welcomed him in.

"Having a cup of tea?" he said, sniffing the air. "What is that, potting soil? Interesting palate."

Marianne laughed. "It's pine and juniper berry. I did add some clodded mushroom, though. Gives it an earthy flavor and it's great for clearing the sinuses."

"Ah. Bit stuffed up, are you?"

Marianne turned her back to him as she went to pour them each a cup. "Something like that," she said.

She didn't add that clodded mushroom was rooting, like the earth, and protective, like their little caps. She didn't mention they made the darkness feel safer. That she hoped inhaling their scent would be the equivalent of listening to a sorrowful violin chord. Resonant and familiar. An expression of gathered color—blues and grays and bruised purples.

Once Artie had his teacup and had scooted back on the sofa so that his legs were sticking out over the edge, he looked at Marianne seriously and said, "So, that was quite the debacle."

She couldn't help it. She threw her head back and laughed, long and hard enough that Artie joined in, drips of brown jumping over the rim of his cup and gathering in his saucer as he bounced with the movement. The more she laughed, the more she realized she might be fighting a bit of hysteria, but she didn't care. It felt good. Everything was in shambles, but Artie was here and Artie was safe and it did— it felt good to laugh.

When the two of them calmed down, they sat in comfortable silence, Marianne watching with a smile as Artie took a delicate sip of his tea. Her smile faded, however, when he said, "Don't think I don't see that bag, Marianne. Are we planning to run away?"

"I'm not sure I'll have much choice in the matter," she said as matter-of-factly as she could, bringing her own cup to her lips.

Artie clicked his tongue in that way of his. "You don't know until you ask! You think that pompous windbag and I haven't had our own share of battles? Of course it's never *my* fault. But you and Glasslight are two peas in a pod. Both bull-headed, to be sure. But I also happen to know your barks are much worse than your bites."

Marianne laughed again. "Are we dogs or bulls in this scenario? Or was it peas?"

"Well, right now you're nothing but a rabbit! Frightening easily and hopping off at the first bit of trouble. But speaking of dogs, you wouldn't think of leaving that poor puppy here all by himself, would you? Pining over my Marianne like a forgotten frog."

Marianne laughed harder. "You really need to straighten out your metaphors, Artie. I officially have no idea what you're talking about."

"Emory, of course! You know—a frog! A frog without his princess. What is the poor boy to do?"

At the mention of Emory's name, Marianne quickly sobered and took another sip of her tea. Until she realized her hand was trembling and set the cup down on her saucer with a *clink*. Buying herself time, she leaned forward and placed the set on the low table next to the tray, then smoothed out her skirts, not looking at Artie as she said, "Emory is not pining over me."

"Is too."

"Is not."

Artie set his own tea down and scooted forward, leveling Marianne with a stare that all but pinned her to the armchair.

"Marianne. My mixed-up Marianne. Forget about our boy for a second. Let's talk about you. You want to run, I can see it. Could see it the moment you turned away back there—and not just because you were sprinting while you did it. But I'm here to tell you you shouldn't. Glasslight pushed you because he believes in you. Not because of some vision, but because of *who you are*. You should stay. Stay and see this thing through. *Fight*. You deserve it. We all do. You can't deprive me of my Marianne now."

"Master Glasslight's visions were never about me, Artie," she said, suddenly exhausted as the words came wrenching from somewhere deep inside her.

But it was true.

She had let herself want this even knowing the inevitability of how it would end from the very beginning. Now, at least, she could be happy for Emory. Maybe that alone would make all of this worth it. "I just happened to be in the wrong place at the wrong time."

Artie shrugged. "Gabriel likes to speak of fate, but we have a hand or two in things. It's your decision, my Marianne."

She shook her head. Her insides felt wrung dry. "I need to help my mother. It would be selfish to stay here."

"From what I understand, Miss Ilya Finch is more than capable." When she didn't respond, Artie added, "You have every right to *want* things, Marianne—to try and dream and compete and yearn. Just for the sake of it! I see your ambition—don't think I don't! You don't yet understand that it's a gift."

Marianne's face scrunched in disgust. Ambition was Jasper Leroux. It was her self-absorbed father, absent from her life. It was Emory trying to be something he wasn't and morphing into a stiff, unfamiliar version of himself in the process. It was selfish. It left hurt in its wake.

Except . . .

She blinked, and Emory's anguished, confused face, framed by roses in bursts of color, swam in her mind. A lingering mark of what *Marianne* had done: abandoning their friendship and never telling him why.

In her effort to curl into herself and hide from all that ugliness, Marianne had done the very thing she hoped to avoid: she had *become* selfish. And she had hurt someone she cared about.

For the first time, Marianne wondered if Artie was right. Maybe she did have it all mixed up in her mind.

My mixed-up Marianne.

Emory was ambitious—she had thought that was his greatest fault. But he was also vulnerable. And kind. Generous, eager to be liked. And it was his insecurities, not his ambition, that had unknowingly ended their friendship. He wanted to please his father. He wanted to please Marianne. He was afraid he never could. And he had left no room for himself. That was his downfall. The very trap Marianne found herself tumbling into now.

No room for herself—no way to tell what she really wanted because she had crammed herself full of insecurities. They were a thousand overstuffed feathers covering up her heart and pricking at her tender skin. Because the sharp, incessant, irritating prods were more comfortable than the bruises that came from real blows.

And Ilya? Marianne had spent years admiring her mother, wanting to be like her—while rejecting the very trait that had built their lives. Ilya's ambition wasn't ruthless; it was resilience. A force that allowed her to create, to give, to endure.

Sitting there, her tea going cold as Artie watched her, Marianne realized one thing: Glasslight and Ilya had been right—she didn't know herself anymore. She had spent too much time smothering her own desires to recognize them when they nudged at her heart.

But here and now, she did know she wanted to stay. She wanted to fight. Whether or not she won, whether or not Glasslight's visions had concerned her, or whether fate was involved. Marianne wanted this for herself.

Lifting her head, Marianne smiled at Artie. A cautious gesture. Another single task she was ready to explore, one slow step at a time. Making her way through a dark forest, upside down and disoriented. But present. And determined.

She tilted her head and examined Artie. "A gift? You really believe that?"

"I've been around a long time, my Marianne. There's darkness and light to everything. It's all about balance. And intention. Generosity can turn noxious in the wrong hands, and stubbornness can be a saving grace. But I know someone who's drawn to the light when I see them. And that's you. It's the only reason I was polite enough not to dump that dreadful concoction into a plant while your head was turned. I know you snuck a spot of potting soil in there, it's the only explanation for the smell," he added, frowning down at his cup on the table.

She bit back a smile. "I promise there's no dirt in my tea."

"Well, whatever it is, I never want anything to do with it again."

"How about I practice?" she said. "Find a brew perfectly suited for you."

Artie made a show of shuddering, making her laugh again. But she considered his words.

Was it possible? Could she embrace the parts of herself that could lead to something good?

After a moment, she smiled, raised her teacup, and waited for Artie to do the same, keeping his arm outstretched so he wouldn't have to inhale the scent. But his eyes twinkled as the two of them clinked together the lips of their delicate, gold-rimmed porcelain.

And in her chest, Marianne felt the sound punctuate a single word:

Go!

16

THE QUEEN

THE NEXT MORNING MARIANNE WALKED straight to Glasslight's office. By now, she was becoming more familiar with the layout of the palace. For although she hadn't explored most of the high-traffic or high-importance areas, she had walked these hallways many times by now, usually in the company of a guard.

But this morning, Marianne had left early enough that the hall outside her room was empty, and no guard felt the need to plaster themself to her side, often assaulting her nose with the potent scent of their rosemary hair wax.

But it seemed that Marianne had overestimated her sense of direction, for she quickly found herself lost, and had to backtrack more than once until she started to recognize the particular wallpaper in a familiar set of hallways.

She was turning into what she hoped was Glasslight's hall when a movement caught her eye.

"Mr. Leroux?" she asked, catching his profile as he stalked out of a room several doors down.

Jasper Leroux turned. "Oh, Miss Finch, how lovely to see you," he said, though the words seemed to convey the exact opposite sentiment.

Marianne looked around. The hallways were empty; it was still quite early. "Are . . . are you visiting Emory?"

Jasper paused for a moment too long. "Yes. Of course," he said, smearing on an amiable smile.

Uneasiness slithered through her. She felt as if she could see the false stiffness that Emory tried to emulate in Jasper's shoulders, and her insides coated with that slick, dark oil she felt whenever she was in Jasper's presence.

They stood in silence for the length of a heartbeat, until it was clear neither of them had any interest in prolonging the conversation.

"Did you need directions?" she finally asked. "Emory's room is—"

"No, no. I've been here several times, Miss Finch," he said with a haughty laugh. "I know my way around perfectly well. I have plenty of other acquaintances to pay my respects to besides my son. I assure you," he took a step closer, "you shouldn't trouble yourself with me."

For a moment, she continued to blink at him, his words hanging in the air, feeling almost like a threat. He didn't move, and she wondered whether he would ask about the letter he had sent. Marianne had thrown it into the trash long ago. But, thankfully, he only offered one more nod before pressing past her.

Her mind snagged on the encounter for the rest of her trek to Glasslight's office.

Was Jasper really visiting acquaintances, or did he have some other business in this area of the palace? Was it possible he was somewhere he wasn't supposed to be? Should she tell someone?

You shouldn't trouble yourself with me.

The words had been layered. They seemed to take on more weight the more she thought about them, until they were digging into the bottom edges of her mind. Definitely a threat.

When she finally found her way to the right section, Marianne forced the interaction out of her thoughts, her nerves reigniting as she remembered that she was up so early to plead for her continued place at the palace. She was here to fight for something she was finally ready to admit she desperately wanted (though she still refused to think past the end of the summer). Something that had nothing to do with Jasper Leroux.

Glasslight's office occupied almost an entire turret of the palace, with windows three stories high overlooking the sprawling grounds. When she arrived, the door was closed, and Tiago was painstakingly pacing back and forth in front of it. Inside, she heard the low hum of voices.

"Oh no," Marianne said, clicking her tongue like Artie and bending down to pick the tortoise up. "Did you get locked out of the important meetings?"

She sat in one of the chairs lining the hall and used the tip of her finger to stroke Tiago's smooth, porcelain shell, feeling the raised outlines as she cradled it in her lap.

It seemed as if the patterns were hand painted, with floral designs edged in gold. The tortoise turned its head so that it appeared to be looking at Marianne, leaning into her touch eagerly, its white crystalline coating shimmering in the light of the sconces lining the hallway. The material of his shell was bumpy and rough, with a texture almost like sugar. For just a moment, Marianne let herself sink into the wonder of holding magic between her hands. Tiago clearly was enjoying it. The tortoise sank down, folding its stubby legs and lifting its head in pleasure as she scratched beneath its chin like a dog.

It was only a few minutes before the door opened. She stood, setting Tiago back on the ground where he immediately set to work making his way into Glasslight's office.

The person coming out nearly tripped over his steady, rhythmic movements, so Marianne had to whisk Tiago out of the way before she looked up and discovered Emory emerging through the door.

"Oh!" he said, looking a bit dazed. "Good . . . good morning."

"Good morning," Marianne said.

They blinked awkwardly before Emory gave a quick bow of his head, letting his dark hair, which hadn't been styled for the day, fall into his face. He circled around Marianne, giving her a rather wider berth than strictly necessary and walked down the hall, his back ramrod straight, until he disappeared from sight, never once looking over his shoulder.

Perhaps he was feeling embarrassed after their moment of closeness in the rose garden yesterday, though she was surprised to discover that no such emotion took up residence in her own body.

On the contrary, she had felt a thrill in her chest at the sight of him. Then again, it was Emory who had shown his vulnerability, while she stood close-lipped and stubborn as ever. Did he regret confiding in her? She recalled the way her heart had thrummed and her skin had tingled. The feel of his chest beneath her palm . . .

Marianne shook the memory away and turned to the open door.

Maybe, after her apology to Glasslight, she would manage to find one for Emory. She realized she hated the thought of him slipping away, retreating into himself the same way she had.

Inside Glasslight's office, a tight spiral staircase led to another landing, which Marianne assumed housed his sleeping quarters. But at the moment, Glasslight was standing behind his enormous wooden desk, sorting through a pile of papers and muttering to himself. Today, his long, silvery beard was simply combed, and he still appeared to be in his night clothes—silk, like most of his attire, and striped, with a plain emerald-green robe hanging open over the top.

"Master Glasslight?" Marianne said, stepping farther into the room.

The morning sun lit everything in bright golds—all of Glasslight's shelves filled with knickknacks, books, and strange-looking instruments. And, of course, the odd assortment of bones peeking out here and there.

Glasslight looked up. "Ah, there you are, my dear girl. Did Emory fetch you? I must say, that is some impressive speed."

"No, I was already here. I wanted to—"

"Good woman. Never mind how you came to be here, so long as you are."

Marianne gave a half-hearted smile. She sat without being asked and nervously started straightening the corner of Glasslight's map showing the kingdom's ley lines.

She was quite familiar with the map, since she had spent a full day carefully drawing a sketch replica and labeling each line and area in the kingdom with which it was associated. It contained a threaded map of lines Glasslight was certain retained some sort of magical current.

She adjusted it where it sat on the desk, lightly fiddling with the thin thread.

Before she had a chance to gather the courage to speak, Glasslight went on distractedly: "Now, as I was just telling Mr. Leroux, unfortunately, I shall have to suspend our lessons."

Marianne's finger slipped as her heart sank. One of the threads came loose in the process, unraveling several others in its wake. She hurriedly looked up at Glasslight, who was busy reading a lengthy parchment, and started to rearrange the threads on the map, curving them around the upright pins.

So, she was too late.

The heaviness of her disappointment took her by surprise, nearly knocking the wind from her as she frantically wound and rewound the thread, muttering under her breath for it to cooperate, reminding herself of the morning she had met Glasslight—the morning she had spent in her mother's workshop before everything changed.

But she wouldn't give up so easily this time. She wouldn't run and curl in on herself. She wouldn't shut anyone out. Perhaps Glasslight's mind could yet be changed.

Keeping her eyes on the map, she said, "M-Master Glasslight, please. I'm here to apol—"

"Leave that be, will you?" Glasslight said, staring down at her hands in horror. "It's starting to look like a Jackson Pollock painting."

"A what?"

"Never you mind. Wrong world. Wrong time. Just put the thread down and step away," he said, shooing her with his hands.

"But I can—"

"Anyway, as I was saying," he said, setting the thread down and going back to his parchment, "I've been called on some urgent business. Shouldn't be more than a fortnight at most I'll be away. In the meantime, Artie will take over your instruction. Though I'll warn you, it won't be nearly as interesting. Neither the man himself nor his expertise. I've tried to hammer into him a little charm or something of the like, but the poor man's stuck in his ways."

Marianne blinked. Wait . . . "You're . . . you're not sending me home?"

Glasslight looked up from the papers on his desk, his violet eyes sharp. "Sending you home? Whatever for?"

"Well, after yesterday . . ."

He paused. "Yesterday? Now, now, what kind of a mentor do you take me for? You think I would ship you off after a tiny bout of insolence? You're young! And a fool, that much I'm convinced of, but all that will wring itself out with a bit of age and experience. You've got spark, my dear girl. And spirit. If I can find a way to nudge you in the right direction, that will mean a whole lot more than anything I could hope to *teach*. I wouldn't throw something so rare out the window. Mr. Leroux was right in that regard."

Marianne, too stunned to speak, only sat staring, prompting Glasslight to stand to his full height, placing his arms behind his back and smirking down at her over the desk.

"Heart and soul, that's what you are, Marianne Finch. My visions may be a bit murky, but I never jump into something without a bit of due diligence. You have a surprisingly large circle of friends, my girl. Nearly everyone in that stodgy hamlet you call home had a story to tell! Granted, many of them haven't spoken to you in several years, but they were still bursting with glowing remarks. Long-winded remarks—it seems they're all starved for even the most minor bit of excitement; so you can imagine what they felt when I knocked on their doors! But glowing, nonetheless.

"You see, you'll soon come to understand how important it is, in my position, to prepare enough to cultivate faith in both myself and any project I undertake. In the good it will do. Because that's the only thing that really matters. And now, more than ever, I can safely say I also have faith in you."

A swell of emotion was clogging Marianne's throat as he finished speaking. She looked down quickly, trying to blink away the sting of tears. He had spoken to the people of Silver Edge? Who? What had they said about her? Marianne could hardly believe anyone had something so good to report. Not after she had locked herself away for six years . . .

But really, she supposed, it wasn't so long ago that she was going door to door herself. Asking to borrow books, to fix random contraptions. There was a time when Marianne knew everyone in Silver Edge by name. And though they sometimes grumbled when they'd discover Marianne surrounded by every piece, wheel, gear, and fragment of their carefully disassembled belongings, they always had a smile for her. And she for them.

Glasslight walked around the desk and gently tapped a thick finger on the bottom of her chin. She lifted her gaze, staring at him squarely. He smiled.

"I mean it, Miss Finch. This marvelous brain is good for more than a few magic tricks," he said, tapping the side of his head. He wasn't wearing a hat today, and his hair was short-cropped, silvery, textured, seeming to glow in the sunlight streaming through the windows.

"This is worthwhile, what we're doing here. Bigger than any of us. My visions never lie. A leader, that's what I saw. Someone with reach across the kingdom—across *worlds*. Soon enough you'll see it too."

* * *

It turned out, Glasslight had one more surprise up his sleeve before he set out later that day.

After being summoned alongside Emory, Marianne and he were led for the first time down one side of a grand double staircase and back into the palace's foyer. Marianne hadn't been there since her arrival, and she marveled at the enormous ceilings painted with as much color and detail as some of her mother's most expensive tapestries.

Once there, they turned right and were led down a hall to another spacious room, where they were told to wait.

As soon as they were alone, Marianne turned to Emory. He was facing away from her, examining an entire wall of gigantic paintings. They seemed to be mostly of the royal family throughout history, along with a few horses. Before she could talk herself out of it, she reached out a hand and grabbed Emory's arm, pulling him to face her. His eyes widened in surprise.

"Emory," she said, seizing upon their time alone, and giving voice to a suspicion that had been brewing since his formal nod several minutes ago and careful avoidance of her eyes as they walked here together. His strange behavior came down to more than just their discussion in the rose garden yesterday, she was sure of it. Something else was going on, and Marianne intended to find out what it was.

"What were you and Glasslight discussing?" she said.

This seemed to catch him off guard. "What?"

Keeping her fingers around his arm, she moved closer, breathing in the scent of fresh laundry and mint. "This morning, when I ran into you outside Glasslight's office. Why were you there so early?"

"Why—we—" Emory closed his mouth, staring at her with an inscrutable expression, sizing her up. "Master Glasslight was just informing me of his plan to go. He summoned me. The same as you."

Marianne didn't answer. Something wasn't adding up. Glasslight hadn't summoned Marianne—he had claimed that was where Emory was going when he left. And now something in Emory's behavior was . . . off.

But there was no time to dwell on it, for at that moment the door opened and Marianne dropped Emory's arm, turning to the double doors.

Several guards marched in, followed by a regal woman in a floor-length gown. She had dark, tightly coiled curls wrapped in an elaborate updo, and a silver tiara perched on her head.

"Your Majesty," came a familiar voice, and Marianne watched as Glasslight trailed the queen into the room, pushing past the guards standing in his way with a scowl before beaming at Marianne and Emory.

"May I present my proteges? You've heard much about them already, of course. This is Marianne Finch"—Marianne curtsied, reluctantly tearing her awed gaze away from the woman's angled face and penetrating almond eyes—"and Emory Leroux," Glasslight finished.

Emory bowed beside Marianne. The queen dipped her chin, smiling pleasantly. She moved forward until she was close enough to grasp each of their hands in turn.

"A pleasure," she said. Her voice was husky and smooth, her skin dark and beautiful. "I have great faith in Glasslight here, and he seems to see quite a bit in the two of you, from what I hear."

Marianne felt herself flush. She felt light as air, almost desperate to be holding the queen's hand again, just so she could be sure she wouldn't float away.

As a child, Marianne used to dream of meeting the queen. The woman in front of her was barely sixteen when she took over the throne, but Marianne had read anything she could get her hands on that came out about her, awed that a girl so close to her own age—barely more than ten years her senior—could have so much responsibility. So much opportunity and respect.

"The pleasure is ours, of course," Emory said, reminding Marianne that she had been standing mute.

"Yes," she agreed a bit too quickly. "We appreciate your hospitality and the guidance of Master Glasslight. And the palace is lovely."

She went on, now somehow unable to stop talking. "Just yesterday I found the most charming rose garden. It reminded me of home. Not that we have anything so spectacular, but we keep some herbs and flowers, especially for teas. I know you have ingredients for some incredible teas in the palace grounds. Just yesterday I made a brew that, well, Artie, you know, the royal archivist? He wasn't a fan. But normally my teas are . . . well, I'll work on them. My mother, she's really the one with the gift. She can just look at someone and tell precisely what blend they need in that very moment."

Now that she had opened her mouth, Marianne couldn't seem to stop talking. It was very unlike her.

Next to her, Marianne noticed Emory smirking. And though she could have elbowed him in irritation, she was at least relieved to see some of his strangeness melting away. Marianne, on the other hand, was starting to make a fool of herself. Her eagerness was making her face flush. What would the queen think if Marianne couldn't stop herself from prattling on nonsensically? She tried to remember the queen was just a woman.

A woman with immense power and authority . . . and a track record of ending wars . . . negotiating landmark treaties . . . all when she was younger than Marianne was now.

Finally, Marianne managed to trail off. She took a great gulp of air, snapping her mouth shut with an audible click.

The queen, to Marianne's shock, was smiling down at her, amusement dancing in her eyes. It reminded Marianne of the image she had seen of the two of them in Glasslight's mirrored hall—with the queen laughing, it had seemed, at a joke Marianne had made. Now, it wasn't quite a laugh on the queen's lips, but she was wearing an expression that warmed Marianne's chest with pride nonetheless.

A moment later, when Glasslight dismissed them and mentioned that Artie would arrange for their first shadowing of his duties, Emory said, "I haven't heard you talk that much in years."

At that, Marianne did elbow him. Holding his side and wincing, he said, staring at her out of the corner of his eye, "I didn't say I didn't like it."

Marching ahead, Marianne did her best to hide her smile.

17

THE ROYAL ARCHIVE

ARTHUR WINTHROP, ROYAL ARCHIVIST, WAS said to have the most extensive knowledge of the Kingdom of Wyn for six generations. He could recall any date, figure, or location of significant events from *memory*, as well as point anyone toward any artifact they were hoping to find—from royal correspondence, to sacred relics, to smashed pieces of armor from famous battles, based on nothing more than two or three vague words of description.

He was particular about designing exhibits, organizing official tours, and training each member of his nearly one-hundred person staff. He could recite the entire genealogical history of the royal family—and most noble lineages—back nearly twelve generations, he could translate from twenty different languages without the help of a single book, and he insisted on resealing every single treaty, alliance, decree, or edict in the entire sprawling archives every ten days.

Marianne and Emory were both quite familiar with this last one, as it had taken them the majority of their first week Glasslight was away assisting in this very process. In that time, Emory's strangeness faded to the point that Marianne wondered if she had imagined it. It had been early, and Glasslight was leaving; he had opened himself to her and she had walked away. Of course Emory was acting peculiar. She still felt a stab of guilt when she thought of their time in the rose garden.

Since then, they had been friendly—friends, even. The way it used to be. But she noticed a new formality in Emory's behavior toward her, and it made her strangely sad. Though she didn't know how to break through it. She wasn't brave enough to try.

It was odd, not hearing Artie (*Master Winthrop*, Marianne reminded herself; now that she was under his instruction, it was quite inappropriate to refer to him as anything else) speak of magic in the entire two weeks Marianne and Emory spent shadowing him, as it had previously seemed to be his primary interest. Though that was not to say their temporary mentor didn't speak of anything.

Quite the opposite. Master Winthrop didn't seem to *cease* speaking in the several hours a day they were with him.

As he gave them tours and introduced them to members of the royal council (Artie didn't seem to share Glasslight's desire to keep them bound to menial tasks). He talked ceaselessly throughout history lessons, late-night indexing, and research requests from visiting scholars.

And Marianne listened raptly to every single word.

As she followed Artie, she thought of the days she had spent gathering books from her neighbors in Silver Edge. All the hours she had spent reading up on eliminating garden slugs, training a particularly stubborn mule, and polishing silver had kept her fascinated—but it was nothing compared to the battles, diplomatic missions, and power struggles Artie filled them in on here.

After their long sessions with Artie, Emory would knock on her door at night, and they would stay up for hours discussing everything they had learned, with Emory helping Marianne fill in gaps in her notes as she crowded page after page with all of her discoveries. More than once she fell asleep on the couch, only to wake and find Emory gone, a blanket pulled over her shoulders and their tea from the previous evening tidied away (she was getting better at her brews—Emory preferred a hibiscus and pine blend, while Artie stuck to plain mint).

All in all, Marianne was torn when Glasslight finally returned—not after two, but three full weeks—speaking of their next magical task. The thought filled her with a thrill of excitement, but Artie and his books and bright smile had made her days truly joyful.

Emory seemed equally taken with their work in the archive, filling his own room with stacks of history books and scrolls laden with the kingdom's most archaic and unpredictable policies. (Emory particularly liked the mandatory nap time one royal archivist instated more than two centuries ago, as well as the "squirrel safeguard," meant to protect squirrels from falling into the large holes made by the palace's drawbridge.)

But now Glasslight was back, and he had plans.

"The palace is hosting a ball," Glasslight announced the morning after his arrival. Marianne and Emory were seated on the floor of his office, copying a set of royal edicts Artie had lent out from the archive so that they could prepare to sit in on a meeting with a chancellor from a visiting kingdom.

At first, Marianne didn't hear Glasslight, as she was too busy scolding her parchment for refusing to sit flat. She looked up. "What?"

"A ball," Emory said, tapping Marianne on the ear with his quill.

Glasslight nodded. "Mm. A perfect opportunity for my protégés to mix and mingle, learn the art of introductions, dealing, the like."

Marianne paused. "No magic?"

Glasslight looked appalled. "Magic? At a royal function? What do you take me for?"

"So it's not another task?"

"I didn't say that," Glasslight said, a twinkle in his eye.

Though she went back to copying the edict from the scroll in front of her, Marianne kept glancing at Glasslight. Their talk before his trip had eased most of Marianne's worries, but she couldn't help but wonder whether she had put him off of using magic to try and teach his lessons.

When she came here, all Marianne wanted was to make an important connection, maybe satisfy a bit of curiosity, and make her mother happy—hopefully change Ilya's perception so that she no longer saw Marianne in that gray, flat, unflattering light she had over the past few years.

Now, Marianne found herself wanting . . . more. She wanted to please Glasslight and learn more about his vision. Both the magical one that had led him to Marianne and Emory, as well as the potential he claimed to see in her. His vision of who Marianne could become. Both he and Emory —and Ilya, for that matter—spoke of a version of Marianne she longed to find. Over the last several nights, she had gone to sleep seeing the mirrors in that hall again, this time in a new light. The image of herself exploring the streets of Queensmont and organizing her own home.

Kissing Emory.

"In any case," Glasslight continued, "You two can't possibly be trusted to get yourselves ready for such an event. I shall send the royal seamstress this evening. The ball is in four days' time. Hopefully she can prepare something suitable for you both by then. We'll be hosting delegates from several kingdoms, as well as welcoming a slew of nobility and other subjects. It will be good for you to get a feel for these types of functions and the best way to engage with people from all places and backgrounds."

Glasslight was pacing behind his desk, his massive silhouette moving back and forth in front of the towering windows. Not for the first time, Marianne wondered if he knew more than he had let on about what he had seen in his vision. Did he really, truly believe Marianne would be a leader? Even that was a frustratingly vague concept. She might lead as part of the council for the royal palace, as Glasslight did—or she might lead a group of ten-year-olds on a tour up Cascade Peak.

Of course, that wouldn't explain his insistence that his apprentice would someday influence the entire kingdom—and, she marveled once again, worlds beyond.

Doing her best to quell the uncertainty, she refocused on copying the edict, her mind already spinning on the possibilities that would open after she won whatever task Glasslight hand in mind for them at the ball.

18

THE DRESS

A CHALLENGE TO MARIANNE'S PLAN of keeping
steady and cool in the face of their next task came in the
form of a dress.

Several days after a visit from the seamstress (during
which the terse, unsmiling woman measured seemingly every
possible length of Marianne's body), Emory knocked on her
door holding a large and beautifully wrapped package, and
wearing a ridiculously emphatic grin.

"I come bearing gifts!"

For a moment, Marianne only stood mute, staring
between Emory's face and the elaborate bow on top of the
box in his arms.

He laughed. "It's from Glasslight. Your dress for the ball." Nudging his way past Marianne, he said, "My suit came yesterday. A bit frilly for my taste, but it ought to get the job done."

Marianne pictured Glasslight's colorful silk trousers and the bright ribbons he had tied in his trailing beard the day before. For the first time, it occurred to her to be nervous about what the seamstress may have put together. Marianne had been hopeful, after observing most of the clothing worn around the palace. But Glasslight had a very particular style —vibrant, much like the room Marianne was currently staying in—and if he had directed the seamstress . . .

Wanting to either learn the horrible truth or ease her concerns, she ripped the package out of Emory's arms and set it on the bed, tearing through the layers of paper inside until she came upon a bit of lace and silk. She looked at Emory apprehensively and then pulled the dress free, sweeping it out and holding it against her body, watching the hem kiss the carpeted floor.

Her wide eyes found the long mirror tilted against the wall first, and then Emory. "What . . . is this?"

He smirked. "Seems as if the seamstress didn't need Glasslight's help after all."

Marianne shook her head. That's not what this was. It was more than talent or intricate skill. She had seen the likes of that more than enough in Ilya's workshop.

This was something else entirely.

She swished the skirt, watching the soft silvery-cream material shimmer in the light of the candles lining the room. It was like looking at the moon. It reminded her of the pearls of light that had come from the mirrored hall. Lace crept up the bodice and along the hem, and the sleeves that came to her elbows flared out.

Looking in the mirror again, Marianne caught Emory watching her. They locked eyes and she spun to face him. He held her gaze for another beat before dropping it down to the dress. "He did give it a little something extra. No one will understand why exactly, but they'll be . . . drawn to you." Something in his eyes shifted when he said it. They darkened, heating as they traveled across Marianne's face.

"Drawn to me? Magically? I thought Glasslight said he would never use magic at a royal function?"

He shrugged one shoulder, his playful smile returning, until his eyes roved down the dress once more, after which he swallowed, his voice turning deep as he cleared his throat and said, "Your . . . or, I mean, *our* task is to talk with as many people as attractiv—uh, achievable." His face turned red. "You know high-ranking or . . . otherwise. Ahem. All while using the knowledge from the edicts we've studied with Glasslight, along with what we learned while shadowing Artie," he finished quickly.

"Glasslight said he'd check up with everyone we spoke to to find out what they thought and what we discussed. The individual who's had the most useful and relevant conversations by the end of the night wins."

Marianne smiled, amused by Emory's obvious fluster. Though she did wish she could quiet the voice in her mind that told her it was only because of the magic woven into the dress she was holding against her.

She slowly folded it over her arm and walked past Emory toward the couch, draping it over the back. She could feel Emory's eyes following her, prickling the skin of her neck, and nearly felt the graze of his arm as she passed close-by. When she faced him again, he was blinking rapidly, shaking his head.

She laughed. "The magic seems to work, then? I didn't even have to put it on."

There was a flush creeping up Emory's neck, but his face was serious. When he spoke, it was barely more than a whisper. "I don't need any help noticing you, Marianne."

Her smile slowly fell as the breath in her chest constricted. She was standing closer to him now, pressed against the sofa. She could feel the carved top digging into her lower back as she curled her fingers around the wood, tightening her grip to stop them from trembling. Nervous, she didn't want to break the moment. This close she could smell the soap on his clothes, see the heat in his eyes. Ever since their time in the rose garden, she had wanted to be near him again. Alone. She had wanted to see him looking at her like that.

Marianne watched him for exactly one heartbeat. Then she bunched her nervousness into something resembling courage and pushed onto her tiptoes, pressing her mouth to his.

At first it was soft. And perfect. A single moment before she pulled away. But Emory came with her, drawn forward, almost losing his balance in the sudden gap between them, and she smiled. He reflected it back with a dazzling grin of his own before she felt his fingers lift to her waist, one hand, then the other.

And then, as if he couldn't take another second of waiting, he pulled her in again, his lips meeting hers, digging his fingers into her sides. With that, she became lost, feeling more awe than she had when faced with any magic.

For a moment, he broke the kiss, just long enough to dip his forehead to hers, move his hand to her chin, rub the pad of his thumb across her cheek.

"Marianne," he murmured softly. The only answer she gave was to wrap her hands around his neck and pull him in for more.

19

THE BALL

MARIANNE'S STOMACH FLUTTERED WITH
NERVES as she opened the door to her room. Glasslight
had arranged for someone to style her hair and assist with
the moonlight dress, but in spite of all the help and
expertise, she felt self-conscious. The only other time she had
worn a dress this elaborate was when her mother made her
one for her fifth birthday. Now she thought of it, that one
had been similar to the dress she wore now.

Because she loved her mother and because Ilya's work
was beautiful in any form, Marianne had put it on right
away, wearing a big smile. But Ilya had taken one look at her,
shaken her head, and chuckled.

"Oh, my girl. I had a feeling. But I dreamed of this dress the other night and it was too beautiful a design to ignore."

Marianne had looked down at the skirt. Woven with blues and purples, it had threads of gold and scenes of stars stitched into the hem. It was more than beautiful, it was breathtaking. But Ilya was laughing. "It looks lovely on you, my Marianne, but not quite right, hmm?"

Letting out a breath of relief, Marianne had agreed.

After giving it one more twirl to watch the blend of colors ripple as the soft skirt flowed around her like water, she had repackaged it and left it on the step of Eliza Snell, watching and giggling with Ilya from the bushes as the young girl opened it and started to shout with joy.

Every time Eliza wore the dress—which was once a week until she outgrew it—Marianne had smiled, relishing the warmth that filled her chest.

Back then, Marianne now realized with a pang, she had known herself so much better. It had only taken a moment to recognize what fit and what didn't—and what she might want instead.

Well. At the very least, she knew she wanted to win.

Emory did a double take when she opened the door. And even though there was a bit of muddled cloudiness as the magic in the dress went to work, this time she didn't mind. Only the day before she had been able to memorize the look in his eyes—wanting, wonder, affection—when the only thing in front of him was Marianne.

"You look . . ." he trailed off.

Marianne smiled. "So do you."

His suit was dashing and perfectly tailored, made of a midnight blue material and soft to the touch. Though, even after taking a moment to look for it, she wasn't sure she could detect the magic Glasslight had surely woven in.

She paused, scanning him up and down, waiting to feel the same cloudiness she saw in Emory's eyes, but it never came.

"Shall we?" he said, offering an arm and pulling Marianne out of her thoughts.

For the first time, she noticed something else in his expression. It wasn't just the strange cloudiness in his eyes, but a stiffness in his movements, some of the formality she had come to understand meant Emory was doing his best to hide something.

"Is everything okay?" she asked, taking his arm as they made their way to the ballroom. "You look like Artie when in the presence of clodded mushrooms."

Emory gave a half-hearted smile. "I'm fine."

"Emory." When he didn't stop or look over at her, Marianne came to an abrupt halt, forcing him to do the same. She was surprised to see his face pained and pinched. "Emory, what is it?"

His shoulders drooped. "It's nothing. Honestly. My father . . ."

Marianne stiffened, a mixture of distaste and apprehension pricking her uncomfortably. "Your father? Did he send a letter? Is everything all right?"

Shaking his head, Emory said, "He's here. We just had a bit of a . . . it doesn't matter. I wish he hadn't come, but there's nothing I can do about that now. Marianne," he suddenly took her hands in his, his tone turning oddly urgent. "Please stay away from him."

She drew her head back in surprise. "What?"

"If he tries to talk to you tonight, just ignore him. With that dress you should have plenty to keep you occupied."

Unease crept over Marianne's skin. Why would Jasper Leroux try and speak with her? And why was he here? "Emory, what's going on?"

He tilted his head, examining her. "Are you nervous, Marianne?"

"What?" she said, caught off guard.

His eyes crinkled with affection. "You've unraveled about a foot of thread from my jacket," he said, looking down.

Marianne followed his gaze to find several loops of Emory's gold thread wrapped around the finger she had near the sleeve at his wrist. "Ah!" she exclaimed, flinching as she ripped the thread away.

Emory laughed. "There's nothing to worry about, Marianne. You're going to be brilliant."

Torn between a bloom of warmth at his words and annoyance at the obvious change of subject, Marianne took a breath and said, "Emory—"

But just then, a booming voice at their backs made both of them jump. "Aha! My extraordinary proteges!"

They turned to see Glasslight making his way toward them, wearing an ensemble made entirely of silk, including a bright purple cloak that trailed along the floor behind him. "I trust Mr. Leroux passed along the expectations for tonight's task?" he said, addressing Marianne.

She nodded mutely, keeping her gaze on Emory, but he was smiling again, and had taken several steps away from her.

She didn't find another opportunity to speak with him, as Glasslight, obviously not trusting Emory had done the job well enough, went on to describe the rules for the ball himself: Speak to as many individuals as possible. Stay on topic—royal policies, current affairs, attractive aspects of their history. Glasslight would follow up, and whichever apprentice had racked up the most relevant and cumulative conversations at the end of the night would win.

As this was their third official task—the first of which had ended in Marianne's triumph (with her six phoenix feather victories over Emory's three), and the second of which had been won by Emory (collecting the most moments in the mirrored hall)—Marianne would need to win tonight in order to secure the full apprenticeship.

The thought made her jittery.

She had been nervous before, but also excited. Now though, with Emory's odd behavior and the specter of Jasper and something he may or may not want to say to Marianne looming over her, it was harder to summon the fierce determination she had felt before leaving her chambers only moments ago.

She had wanted to playfully banter with Emory before they entered the ballroom. She had wanted a kiss of good luck as they parted ways. She had wanted to lock eyes with him throughout the evening, gaining confidence as the night wore on, sure she would beat him fair and square . . .

Once they entered the ballroom, Emory split off, though Marianne kept an eye on him, watching for an opportunity to finish their conversation while also scanning the room for Jasper Leroux. Thankfully, there didn't seem to be any sign of him yet.

"Ready, my girl?" said Glasslight.

Marianne forced her gaze from Emory, locking with Glasslight's violet eyes. There was something there she didn't recognize, and it only added to her nerves. She started to nod, then—

"Master Glasslight, is something going on?" she asked abruptly.

He blinked at her. "Always. I am the royal advisor! This is the palace! Something's always afoot!"

"I mean . . . you and Emory, is—"

"Ah! The ambassador from Hartshire. I'm afraid I can't leave her waiting. Until the end of the evening, Miss Finch! May it be a magical one," he added with a wink before sweeping away, leaving Marianne standing with her mouth open, the unfinished question dangling from her lips.

She was wondering whether there was any ambassador at all or if Glasslight had whisked away simply to avoid her questions, when Artie rushed up in a bounce of white hair and bushy beard.

"Oh, my dear, my Marianne! You look *wonderful*," he said, taking her hand in between both of his and patting her fingers enthusiastically. Marianne was forced to bend down a bit in order to accommodate the difference in their heights

"Though I may have mentioned to Glasslight that he seems to be losing some of his subtlety. Even I could smell the magic on your dress the moment he showed it to me. Pay no mind, of course, if he tells you I said so, I'm only having a bit of fun. Can't let the old boy get too cocky, eh?" At this, Artie started to cackle and wheeze, and Marianne couldn't help but join in, some of her nerves softening at the edges.

She gave him a quick kiss on the cheek and then stood to her full height, scanning the room for her first target. Above her, the ceiling reflected the candlelight with thousands of painted golden stars.

It was time to focus. No more thoughts of Jasper Leroux or Emory's strangeness or Glasslight's evasive maneuvers.

She was here to complete a task. She was here to win.

Maybe Artie was right about the lack of subtlety, for her enchanted dress seemed to go to work instantly. Within moments, Marianne found herself surrounded by a group of nobles, more than one of whom asked her to dance.

She obliged easily, steadying her racing heart and trying to remember what she had learned under the tutelage of both Artie and Glasslight.

After several dances, she spoke with a visiting ambassador from the nearby Kingdom of Stelbynne, a woman with bright round eyes and a mound of dark hair. Every so often, she was able to catch a glimpse of Emory deep in conversation with someone new, always laughing and smiling, sweeping his dark hair out of his face and adjusting the top button of his shirt.

Marianne caught his eye once and his smile changed instantly, softening like butter. She wondered how she had ever found him off-putting.

When she passed near enough to hear his conversation, it became apparent he was well-connected, as nearly everyone seemed to both know him and like him. They joked and reminisced and Marianne felt a hollow little pang, wishing she could be speaking with only him tonight. Wishing she hadn't spent years avoiding his company.

At one point, very late in the evening, as the hands on her waist became tiresome and the conversation repetitive, the queen finally made her entrance, followed by several guards and members of her court.

Marianne caught her breath, as in awe as ever of the woman's magnificent presence. Looking at her was like beholding one of Ilya's tapestries—she was splendidly beautiful, her dress and braided hair woven and blooming like an intricate work of art.

Marianne's partner, whose name she couldn't remember, dropped her hand and bowed to the queen as she passed. Marianne curtsied politely, but her gaze traveled upward when she noticed the queen's jeweled shoes had stopped moving directly in front of her.

"Miss Finch," the queen said, smiling.

"Your Majesty?" Marianne hadn't meant for it to come out as a question—especially one on which her voice squeaked in excitement. She flushed and cleared her throat. "I mean, hello, Your Majesty."

The queen smiled, glancing at Marianne's dance partner, a sixty-something man whose gray mustache had been stained purple from the punch. "Where is Mr. Leroux?" she said.

Marianne looked around. She hadn't seen Emory in more than an hour, by her estimation. The realization disappointed her. Was she winning the task? Was he busy charming fascinating and beautiful foreign dignitaries?

"I'm not sure. Likely lamenting the lack of anchovies on the refreshment table," she said, though she quickly worried it may have been an inappropriate response. Was it proper to joke with the queen?

Luckily, she laughed, and Marianne relaxed, thinking something about the gesture was familiar, though she couldn't quite put her finger on it.

"I'll be sure to include the delicacy at our next royal function," the queen said warmly, then she bowed and made her leave.

Marianne smiled, and when she turned back, couldn't help but relish the look of astonishment on her partner's face at the seeming familiarity she shared with the leader of their kingdom.

* * *

After several hours, Marianne's hair was coming loose and her feet were starting to ache, so she excused herself from the dignitary with whom she was speaking and found a bench, bending over to check her shoes.

Her face was flushed from the dancing and her body fatigued, but there was a buzz in her limbs. It had all but eradicated any nerves or uneasiness she might have felt at the start of the evening. She was winning—she could feel it.

Emory was well-liked and connected, but there was simply no way he had had as many conversations as she. And there was no way he had worked as hard to stay on topic. (Not with things like the grand clock, the incredible acoustics, and the room's particularly brilliant airflow design threatening to distract Marianne at every turn; she would figure out precisely how each of those marvels worked later.)

In the meantime, she pictured the look on his face when Glasslight announced the results at the end of the night. Somewhere deep in her bones, she knew there would be no anger—an emotion that seemed mostly unfamiliar to Emory —and very little disappointment.

On the contrary, Emory would be thrilled for her. She could picture his gigantic grin, and the way he'd lift her into the air, spin her around. He had wanted her to try, to reclaim herself. He believed in her.

Throughout the evening, she had a response for every question, every remark. Her knowledge of the kingdom was coursing through her and, for the first time in as long as she could remember, Marianne felt as if she was truly in her element.

As a girl, Marianne hadn't simply stolen her neighbor's books and locked herself in her room, she now remembered how she had been welcomed into their homes where they would talk for hours. They'd smile when they opened the door to her eager face. When she took apart their belongings, she'd arrange the pieces on the floor of their living rooms and learn about their lives. She'd return their books and have discussions on their favorite subjects.

She knew the names of all Mr. Crockett's children and grandchildren. She knew Emily Wilder loved to read about astronomy and romance. She knew the Martinez family had inherited a collection of clocks from the Duke of Engels.

She knew all of this, but more than that, she *cared*. It was hard to believe that Marianne had spent the last six years trying to convince herself that she didn't.

"You're quite the commodity, Miss Finch. I've been looking for an opportunity to dance with you all evening."

Marianne froze in the act of rubbing her sore foot, slowly trailing her gaze upward.

Jasper Leroux was as dashing as his son, though with streaks of gray in his dark hair and a few more wrinkles on his charming face. The odd stiffness she had seen in him weeks ago, when she had come across him outside Glasslight's office, was gone, replaced by his false, easy smile. He reached his hand down in a silent gesture, willing Marianne to take it.

She watched it for a moment, unsure what to do; some of her buoyant delight slowly settled, like a snow globe that had been sitting for too long.

For years she had hated this man, had blamed him for the choice she had made as a young girl. To stop trying, stop learning, stop *yearning*. And now, the image of Emory filled her thoughts. The way he had described his father when admitting his true feelings for her in the rose garden. The look on his face as he spoke of Jasper—of a fight they had had? Emory had never elaborated—only hours ago.

But Jasper was just a man. Marianne wouldn't let herself be frightened of him.

Taking his hand, she let him help her to her feet and whisk her through the crush of bodies to the center of the dance floor. Eyes followed her, as they had all night. It was a strange feeling, like the stickiness of cobwebs. The attention stuck to her uncomfortably, though it hadn't before now—she simply found herself wishing not to be seen with Jasper.

Because she knew he must be here for a purpose; he wanted something.

When he found a spot he liked, Jasper stopped walking and tugged on Marianne's hand, bringing it to his shoulder and moving her in time with the music.

There was an entire orchestra on the stage, their strings moving in different tempos and rhythms, though as the night wore on, Marianne was beginning to have a difficult time telling one song from the next.

Before, they had simply been a pleasant backdrop to her triumphant final stretch. Now, in the arms of Jasper Leroux, the strings seemed to screech unpleasantly in her ear, the sound too loud as it grated against her skin.

"So," Jasper started, smiling wide enough that Marianne could see the gleam of his teeth, "how are you liking your time at the palace?"

It was an innocent enough question, and yet there was a strain of menace beneath his words as there often seemed to be when Jasper Leroux spoke, and Marianne had the sense that she needed to tread carefully.

"It's been . . . educational," she said, searching for the right word. In truth, there was nothing that could come close to describing the full spectrum of her experience over the past several weeks.

He nodded thoughtfully. "For Emory too. And a struggle, as well."

"Emory's been wonderful. He's brilliant. And perhaps the most well-liked person in the palace," Marianne said defensively.

Jasper laughed. "The boy puts too much energy into such things. I learned long ago it's a waste of time. There's a difference between being liked and being respected. One path opens doors, the other simply turns you into a trod-upon bleeding heart. I know people don't care for me, Miss Finch. But I've managed just fine. A smile goes a long way, whether it's genuine or not. And when it's not, it's much easier to make the important decisions. The unpopular ones. There's only so much room at the top. One can't bring all of their friends along, anyway. Their weight will only drag."

Marianne paused. "That's the most dim-witted thing I've ever heard," she said, throwing the descriptor she had once overheard back in his face.

For a moment, Jasper only blinked. Then he threw his head back and laughed. "Oh, I always liked you, Miss Finch."

"No, you haven't."

He continued to laugh, whirling her around the dance floor. "No, you're right. I haven't. I was delighted when you disappeared from Emory's life. Though it did send the poor boy into quite the tailspin. But I was right! Look at us now, mere weeks after your reappearance. Look where we are."

Marianne's blood boiled. She didn't have to make herself small, but she also didn't have to stand here and expose herself to his cruelty. "And where is that?" she asked, though she had no intention of listening to the answer. She tried to pull her hand out of Jasper's grip, to turn away. But he only held on to her tighter, digging his fingers into her waist.

"Well, think of Emory. It's difficult for a man of his circumstance and caliber—any man, really, with a sense of pride—to have to step aside for a grasping, self-indulgent village girl who's gotten herself in over her head."

Marianne stopped moving. Her heart began to race, the room blurring at the edges, rage and shame battling in her chest. The music around her seemed to slow, blending into a buzz of unpleasant noise.

But it didn't matter what Jasper Leroux thought of her. Not anymore.

"I have just as much right to be here as Emory," she said when she finally found her voice, forcing it to stay even.

Jasper clicked his tongue, as if she were a schoolgirl speaking back to her teacher. He tightened his hands even more, forcing her to keep dancing, and she tugged against him harder. "It's okay. You're still young. It was your mother who ought to have taught you better. You know, it's ironic, I had to teach her a bit of humility too, not so long ago. She's skilled at the loom, I'll give her that. And beautiful. But a bit of mediocre talent and feeble recognition puffed up her ego too much, I'm afraid. She also didn't recognize an offering of goodwill."

Marianne stilled, frowning as she stared at Jasper's smug smile.

She recalled the times over those few months, years ago, when Jasper had frequented Ilya's workshop, always bringing flowers and wearing that charming smile. The way her mother had rolled her eyes, exhaling with relief when he'd finally leave.

And something in Marianne's mind reached for more, as the puzzle pieces seemed to fall into place.

It was shortly after that that the dynamic in the workshop had shifted. Several of Ilya's workers quit, some of her best clients canceled their commissions. Whispers began to follow Marianne.

This time when Jasper tried to pull her along, she stood her ground. "You started the rumor," she breathed, hatred spilling through her veins.

It scorched beneath her skin, and she wished it was hot enough to burn him. She tried tugging away again, but he held her fingers firm.

"There's no reason for you to have to deal with such unpleasantness. Especially at such a young age. You're still moldable. Still reasonable, I think," he said, holding her tightly, "If it simply came down to who could win these magical tasks Glasslight has set for the two of you, I wouldn't be worried. Unfortunately, there are extenuating circumstances. Rather . . . otherworldly ones."

Marianne stopped pulling for a moment as his words sank in.

He knew about their tasks? About the magic? Glasslight's spell had made it impossible for either Marianne or Emory to speak of them. She knew, because she had tried in one of her early letters to Ilya.

She recalled the way her pen had stalled on the page, refusing to move until she shifted her intention, no matter how hard she dug the tip into the paper. She tried until her wrist was sore and she was out of breath from the effort.

But how did Jasper know? Emory couldn't have told him. Besides, Marianne was almost certain he *wouldn't*.

A small look of triumph lit Jasper's features as he watched her expression change. He finally dropped his hand from her waist, though he still held her fingers, smiling and nodding at the people around them as he silently pulled her back through the crowd.

He didn't stop walking until they had gone through a side door and Jasper had pulled Marianne into a small, dark room with sheets pulled over the furniture. Finally, he let her go. She backed away.

Dislike and disgust pulsed sharply through her. Voices filtered through the open door. She should go . . . but something told her he still had a trump card up his sleeve. A piece of the puzzle she needed to know.

"They're lying to you," Jasper said, turning toward Marianne. Half of his face was in shadow, and the easy smile had vanished. "Gabriel Glasslight and my son. You think you're competing for a spot *with* him, but you're not. Several weeks ago, the wizard had another vision. He learned it was you that was destined to lead. He told Emory, who agreed to stay and help guide you; to keep up the ruse that this was a fair fight, though even that idea was always laughable. But tonight? You're not competing with anyone. You're being watched, nudged, and manipulated."

Marianne stood frozen. "His vision was about me?"

"Which only means no matter how poorly you do or how much my son naturally excels, the game is rigged. I urge you to truly think about that, Marianne. Two important men with misplaced and misguided honor, beholden to intangible rules of some kind of sorcery, falling to their knees and shaming themselves all in the name of one naive girl. Are you really happy humiliating them like that? Being their puppet so that they can grab at scraps of recognition while you're expected to balance power well past your abilities?"

Jasper shook his head in mock disappointment. "You don't want this, Marianne. I never took you for selfish."

"You never took me for anything," she spat back.

It was a single thread to hold onto in the jumbled mess of tangles he had just thrown at her feet, but she held to it fast. In all the times he had come to the workshop, trying and failing to court Ilya, Jasper hadn't looked at Marianne once. Since then, he had shown no interest in anything beyond shaming and belittling her.

And yet . . .

"How do you know about all of this?" she asked, her fight suddenly gone. Her knees had become weak, and she leaned on one of the covered pieces of furniture for support.

Jasper studied her. She wondered if he was debating how much to divulge. How much she might need to know in order to just give up and leave.

"People with actual power are privy to things most either don't need or don't deserve to know. I am a member of the village council, and a respected guest at court. I also know my son. And when his letters started arriving, it was clear to me that something significant was being left out. I had long suspected Gabriel Glasslight of harboring magic. I put two and two together, and then a few weeks ago I came to investigate for myself. The day I had the misfortune of stumbling into you in the halls, actually. I saw his visions with my own two eyes, and I read in Emory's own hand, in his journals—coded with whatever spell the advisor has you both under—what I've just told you. I confronted him about it earlier tonight and he confessed, though the stubborn boy refused to help you see reason. It seems you've worked your own kind of sorcery with him." Jasper smiled humorlessly. "Just like your mother."

He held something out, and Marianne cautiously took it. It was a piece of paper, torn from Emory's journal, written in his hand.

It's for the best. It's what she deserves. She was always going to be the better leader. She was always capable of doing more good. And if I can help with that, I will. Even if I have to lie. I'll do it until she won't run.

All at once, Marianne couldn't stand to hear or read another word. Her stomach roiled with betrayal and confusion, anger and disgust and shame. So much shame.

She should have known better. She had seen firsthand what greed and ambition could do, and yet she had fallen into the trap, slipped in so easily it all felt like a dream.

She knew she couldn't take Jasper at his word. She knew Emory and Glasslight would each have their own side of the story.

But that didn't change the fact that they had both agreed to lie to her—and for what? When it came down to it, it was all in the name of *power*.

Glasslight wanted to mold a leader who would gain fame and influence. He wanted to be in control of the strings pulling at Marianne. After all, he was never anything but upfront about his own pride. His fragile, overlarge ego. And Marianne had played right into it.

And Emory . . . Emory wanted to help. He always wanted to help. But that didn't give him the right to deceive her. It had been six years since he laughed with his father, talking about Marianne and the other villagers behind their backs. He ought to be braver by now. He ought not to fall into the same traps, desperate to please everyone, and always at the cost of Marianne—her feelings and desires and will. She needed him to be stronger than that.

And if she stayed, what would she even be fighting for? To be in the company of people like Jasper Leroux and Gabriel Glasslight. People who played games and cut the dead weight of their friends in order to more easily reach the top.

She had been right all along. It was ugly. All of it.

"You're right about one thing," she said after several moments, refusing to look at Jasper. "I don't want it."

Jasper's eyes gleamed with satisfaction, though he tried to tamp down his smile. She didn't even care. She didn't care that he had won; that she had given in. Suddenly, all she wanted was to go home, to see her mother, to be done with all of it. With all of them. No more lying or magic or games. What was it all for, anyway? To achieve . . . more? More and more, endlessly. There would always be more—and it would always be meaningless.

Already dreading the words rising in her throat, she straightened her spine, looked directly at Jasper, and demanded, "Take me home."

20

THE THREAD

MARIANNE HAD JUST LET HER enchanted, pearl-colored dress fall into a pool at her feet when a thought occurred to her.

It was silly and unnecessary, she knew that. But the idea seemed to overtake her like fire until she had gotten it in her head that she couldn't possibly leave until she had managed to procure a spool of the lovely thread that looked like moonlight. To bring back to her mother.

If anyone would appreciate its beauty and craftsmanship, it would be Ilya. The tea ingredients weren't enough. Nothing would be enough. But perhaps this would help.

As fast as she could, Marianne dressed in her traveling clothes and packed up her bag. She wouldn't be sorry to leave the vivid orange and pink room behind, even if she couldn't help but think of Emory when her gaze landed on the sofa and armchairs. Where they had shared their first kiss and all those hours together.

But he had lied to her. That was a fact. And for what? Why keep it from her? Anger simmered low in her gut, but mostly she felt sorrow, thick and cold enough to all but snuff out everything else.

She wished they hadn't left her out. She wished she hadn't been their puppet. Their dancing bear. Was she flighty in their eyes, too naive and incapable of handling the responsibility? Or did they think she was she too greedy, that the power would go to her head?

It didn't matter, because it would never happen. She would leave and Emory could take over the apprenticeship. Glasslight would train him and his visions would alter accordingly.

It didn't take her long to find the seamstress's office. Marianne knew the sound of a weaver's workshop well; even faint, the clicking of the loom seemed to pull her along. She had been right in guessing it would be in the basement, along with the kitchens and laundering spaces.

When she entered, several servants looked up questioningly, but the no-nonsense seamstress who had measured Marianne for the dress came bustling over before Marianne could speak.

"What is it, Mistress Finch?" the woman said. "Has something happened to your dress?"

Marianne shook her head. She explained her hope in coming there, that her mother was a weaver, and when she mentioned Ilya's name, the woman's eyes lit up.

"Ah! Of course. I'd wondered if perhaps you were related. Ilya Finch is a master at her craft. Her work is truly extraordinary. I'd be honored to share."

The woman's demeanor changed significantly after that, becoming eager and bright. Marianne had to explain more than once that she didn't have room for more than a few spools of thread as everyone tried to press their favorites into her hands.

In the end, she left with six vibrant colors—all lacking the magic Glasslight had woven into the dress, but with an allure all their own—and a promise to tell Ilya about the good work being done in the palace.

Though Marianne had always been in awe of her mother, she could hardly believe that women working for the queen herself could look up to Ilya so much. Not just the work she did, but the way she had made a name for herself across the kingdom. Her bustling business and months-long waiting list. And in spite of everything, the glowing joy and pride she felt was nearly enough to make Marianne forget her sadness for a moment.

She stuffed five spools into her bag, keeping the silvery moon one in her pocket. Above her, the last remnants of the ball continued, but Jasper Leroux was waiting for Marianne at the palace's entrance.

She had left her dress neatly folded on her bed, but she had the thread. A simple reminder.

She had almost reached the front doors, her boots echoing around her as she hurried across the marble floor, when someone called her name.

Squeezing her eyes closed, she took a deep breath and spun around, hugging her bag tightly.

"Marianne," Emory said breathlessly, running up to her, "You disappeared. What are you . . . where are you going?"

She took in his face, his wide worried eyes. He moved closer and she resisted the urge to lean into him and let him wrap his arms around her.

"I saw you dancing with my father," he said. "What did he say to you?" He glanced through the doors at the carriage waiting in the drive. A carriage with his family's crest.

Her shoulders slumped. "The truth, Emory."

To his credit, he didn't feign ignorance or bother denying anything. Rather, he grabbed her chin, gently tilting her face up toward him. "Marianne, I told you my father thinks I'm incapable. He believes I'll only amount to something if he steps in and does the work for me."

"Isn't that exactly what you're doing with me?"

Hurt flashed in his eyes. He shook his head, at a loss for words. And then he leaned down and kissed her. Marianne let him, opening her lips and tasting the sweetness of apple cider he must have been drinking at the ball. She could feel the urgency in the way he held her, moving his hand into her hair. Everything he was trying to communicate without words.

"No," he breathed, breaking off and pressing his forehead to hers. "I only wanted . . ." He exhaled, pulling away. "I was disappointed at first. When Glasslight told me it had been you all along. I had wanted to please my father, and I had thrown myself into this . . . all of it. Then I realized, even though Glasslight didn't see it until the magic showed him, *I* did. I was disappointed for myself, but I wasn't surprised. I wasn't resentful. I realized it had been inevitable. Of course it was you, Marianne. I *want* it to be you. Please don't listen to my father. Please don't throw this away."

Marianne looked away from him. She had been right— Emory would have been happy for her.

"Emory . . ." she started, returning her gaze to his—and there it was again. The disappointment. It crowded in his eyes. He knew what she was going to say and that she was letting him down again. It filled her with longing, but also with something else—something surprising: outrage. An outrage that had been living beneath her skin for six years.

She grabbed hold of it.

"Emory, I can't be your ideal anymore. It's just as bad as being your dancing bear," she said angrily.

Confusion colored his features. "What?"

"'Like watching a bear stumble around in a dress.' Isn't that what you told your father all those years ago? You never really expected anything from any of us, just like him. It's only because I pulled away that you built something up in your head, because I wasn't there to live up to it. You were . . ." A sob clutched at her throat, and she took a step back.

"You were my best friend. I shared myself with you in a way I never did with anyone else. And when I heard you describe me like that, it broke my heart, Emory."

Suddenly his expression cleared, and she knew he remembered.

"I . . ."

She shook her head, cutting him off. She knew what he was going to say. He was young, trying to impress his father. He didn't mean it. He wasn't talking about her. But she could still recall Jasper laughing; the sound of him patting his son on the back for his joke.

And she knew it didn't matter. That was the first day she glimpsed that version of Emory . . . The version that he needed to be in order to impress his father. To become like him. A version still in there, ready to submit to Glasslight and do what he was told. And Marianne wanted no part of it.

He looked crestfallen, and she knew her heart was breaking all over again. But it didn't stop her from turning and walking away, through the doors and into the waiting carriage at the bottom of the palace steps.

21

THE SMOKE

Emory

MARIANNE HADN'T EVEN REACHED the door before Emory changed his mind.

He no longer cared about a vision or a winner. He didn't care about pleasing his father or playing along with Glasslight's plans.

As Marianne walked through the palace's front door, he squared his shoulders and took a resolute step forward—only to be stopped by a large, sturdy hand, studded in elaborate rings.

"No, no, my dear boy," Glasslight said calmly.

Scowling, Emory tugged out of his reach, in no mood for Glasslight's nonsense. Where had he come from, anyway?

Glasslight glanced out the doors. "She needs this."

With effort, Emory breathed through his nostrils, trying to steady the hot, unexpected flare of temper in his chest. It didn't happen often, but suddenly he was *angry*.

He was angry at his father and at Glasslight and at this entire charade in which he had ridiculously agreed to participate. Something had clearly happened tonight—something more than Marianne was letting on. And in that moment, Glasslight had no right to claim he had any idea what she needed.

He stood to his full height—not quite matching Glasslight's, but still formidable. "Needs what exactly?"

Glasslight puffed on the pipe hanging from his mouth. He must have stepped out of the ball for a smoke. With another spike of indignation, Emory wondered how much of his interaction with Marianne his mentor had seen.

Glasslight shrugged. "Space. Time. To stand on her own two feet. She needs to figure out what she wants and how to fight for it."

"She can do all of that here. I can help."

Another shrug. "Do what you want, then! Honestly, you imps with your bickering and your wrestling and your outbursts, how much is a man—of my renown, no less—supposed to take? But remember, you agreed to this, boy. You *want* her to excel. The world needs it. It needs her."

Emory's jaw tensed. He looked out the door, an empty space now where she had last stood. He could smell the summer night: the crisp air, cut grass, and gas from the lamps lining the palace's drive. And the lingering notes of Marianne: roses, herbs, fresh linen. Already, it was drifting away, caged up in his father's carriage.

His hands clenched into fists. "Trust me, time with my father will do nothing to help. She deserves better."

Glasslight pulled out a match and took his time lighting his pipe before shaking his fist to fan out the tiny flame. "She can handle it."

Emory paused.

Glasslight was right. Marianne could handle Jasper Leroux. She could handle anything. Emory was the weak one; the one who needed to learn to fight for what he wanted.

When would he? How many times did he have to lose her, to hurt her? How long did he have to love her from afar? How was he supposed to know what to do? Who to please?

For the first time, the answer to that, at least, was clear: He didn't have to please anyone. Because, at last, Emory realized that he could be the kind of man he hoped to be—respectful, agreeable, and good—*without* bending and molding himself.

But where did that leave him? Playing along with Glasslight's grand plans? Giving Marianne space? Easing her open one jagged crack at a time? He was trying, and with each win, her slivers of sunlight shining through were bright enough to scorch him.

Yet, he still craved more, he craved it faster—and he suspected Marianne did, too. If she'd let herself.

"Wipe that look off your face," Glasslight said, puffing out a thick swirl of pink smoke. "And sleep it off. She'll be fine. She'll—"

He cut off abruptly, a strange glassiness slackening his features.

Emory looked over. For the first time, he noticed shapes in the smoke from Glasslight's pipe. He couldn't quite make them out; they were moving fast, flurries and pricks and swirls he didn't understand.

Glasslight met his gaze, slowly pulling his pipe from his lips, and at the expression on his face, Emory's heart began to race, cold dread turning his veins to ice.

He closed the space between them, stepping into the lingering wisps of Glasslight's smoke. "What is it?"

22

THE WITCH

MARIANNE AND JASPER DIDN'T TALK during their journey back to Silver Edge. In fact, they barely saw each other.

Jasper had the good grace to keep his gloating under wraps while he rode on horseback outside of the carriage, which Marianne occupied alone. The only time they crossed paths at all was at night when Jasper would arrange a room for her at the inn they stopped at to rest and water the horses.

During the journey, Marianne mostly looked out the window, fiddling with the spool of silver thread she had brought for her mother.

She took no notes as they passed through Queensmont or the Wandering Hills—a lengthy stretch of land that consisted of low, green hillocks that were said to house fairies. Marianne had borrowed an entire book of fairies from the blacksmith, Mara Gong when she was a girl, reading and rereading the stories. She had never believed in them, of course, though after working with Glasslight, she was no longer so sure.

She felt waves of guilt whenever she thought of Glasslight. In spite of everything, he had believed in her, and she had left without saying goodbye. Then again, it was only a matter of time before Glasslight tracked her down to argue for her return—or to wipe her memories of magic.

The thought made her sorrowful. Though most of her encounters with magic had been terrifying, she wished she could hold on to the moment she had first found the phoenix feather, or the feel of Glasslight's tortoise in her lap, his porcelain shell sparkling and textured like sugar.

They were perhaps an hour outside of Silver Edge when the carriage stopped and Jasper opened the door, handing her another skin of water and a basket with bread, fruit, and cheese. He had kept her steadily replenished with provisions, always on his best behavior when he knocked at the carriage door and greeted her with a smile.

This time, as with all the others, Marianne took the food and water without returning his grin, only offering a mumbled "thank you" as he bowed and closed the door behind him.

Marianne had just drained the last of the water when the outskirts of Silver Edge came into view. It tasted tangy in her mouth, and she wondered whether Jasper had filled it with gooseberries or rhubarb. Maybe even orange slices. The scent was bright and familiar. Perhaps he was trying to atone with added touches of luxury. She wasn't sure why he would bother.

They were on a road that cut through the Mossy Wood —a road she knew well. Within moments they would turn onto a street that led straight to the center of town, which meant she was minutes away from reuniting with her mother. Ilya would smile and hold open her arms and Marianne would fall into them, letting loose every emotion she had refused to feel for the past three days.

At the thought, tears filled her eyes. Marianne forced them back down. She had made it this far, certainly she could hold off until she had exited the carriage and was watching Jasper Leroux recede into the distance.

Still, she shuddered. What would Ilya think when she saw Marianne arrive with him?

Yawning, Marianne put away the empty skin of water and started rewinding the silver thread she had been fiddling with. But she found her vision blurry and her movements jerky. Strangely, she kept missing the spool. She hadn't slept well the last few nights.

That must be the problem, but as her fingertips tingled with numbness, she started to wonder if something else was going on. Was she falling ill? But they were so close. Surely she could last until then. Angelica Martin would have ideas for remedies in her well-stocked cabinets. And Marianne could rest in bed.

But her legs were quickly becoming numb; the world seemed to tilt. Alarmed, Marianne looked up helplessly and out the window, watching as they neared the fork in the road. Less than five minutes. That's all she needed, and then she could ask Angelica for help. Perhaps she would know why black spots were crowding Marianne's vision; why her head was suddenly pounding.

But as they drew closer to the fork, the carriage began to veer left instead of right. Thunder clapped overhead, jarring Marianne in her seat.

"Wha . . ." Marianne tried to ask, moving her hand toward the window, but she found she had little control over her speech, and her body seemed to be moving in slow motion.

She waved her hand curiously in front of her face, wiggling her fingers and then letting her hand drop to her lap. Droplets of rain pelted the glass windows, each one too loud as her head spun.

The last thing she saw was Jasper riding up alongside the carriage, leaning over to peer through at Marianne before she lost consciousness altogether.

* * *

Marianne blinked awake to a dim, narrow room. The sound of rain pounded against stone walls.

A single lamp was lit, winking and sputtering in the middle of the floor. It took time for her eyes to adjust to its light. Her head was aching, and her limbs still felt numb, but also, something else . . . bound. They were bound. At first, Marianne couldn't understand why. The room was dark, and she couldn't see anything binding her feet and hands. But as her eyes adjusted, she recoiled.

They were shadows, like the ones she had seen in the forest. Their dark tendrils were wrapped around her wrists and ankles, holding her to a splintered chair in the center of the room. The more she yanked against them, the more they seemed to tighten, until they were digging into her skin hard enough to bruise and she stopped struggling, breathing hard.

It struck her that the floor beneath her feet wasn't made of wood, but of stone, as were the walls and the ceiling. A single, grubby window next to the door was set into the thick stone, but it showed only darkness outside. How many hours had passed? Night had been falling when Marianne lost consciousness, so there was no way to tell.

She heard a rustle of noises coming from the next room, rising above the sound of the rain, but also something *beneath* it. Something more sinister, like a whisper she couldn't decipher. It seemed to be coming from . . . everywhere—the walls themselves. It crawled across the back of her neck and she wished she had use of her hands to cover her ears and block it out. A constant, low whisper that set her teeth on edge.

The noise in the next room grew louder, and then muffled footsteps on the stone announced the arrival of someone. Marianne's heartbeat kicked up as she watched the doorway, waiting.

Jasper Leroux appeared, a notebook and a box of matches in hand. In the flickering light of the lantern, his face looked serious. Almost . . . regretful.

"You're awake," he said, his voice flat. "I apologize for the dramatics. I sincerely wish there had been another way."

Marianne blinked, uncomprehending. "What . . . what are you doing?"

Her throat clogged as fear wrapped itself around her heart, just as tightly as the shadows around her wrists and ankles. She had been moments away from launching herself into her mother's arms.

The whispers continued, and Marianne suddenly knew they weren't natural, just like the shadows holding her in place.

But even as frightened as she had been in the forest, it was nothing to what she felt now. There, she had known Glasslight was just outside, and Emory was somewhere near. Now she was miles away from both of them.

Even if they did happen to come looking for her, which was unlikely, they'd never find her here in this strange and sinister stone dwelling. For all Ilya knew, Marianne was still comfortable in the palace.

That's when it hit Marianne fully: She was completely alone.

"I told you I have access to certain knowledge," Jasper said, flipping through the notebook in his hand. "Most of the world lives in ignorance, but as a member of a village council, I have the privilege of knowing magic once thrived. Witches and wizards lived among us, wielding their powers as a carpenter might wield a hammer. Of course, I didn't always know this. But as a boy, I spent a great deal of time . . . away from home.

"It wasn't the most welcoming place, you see, and it was best to keep out from beneath my father's foot, so I'd build forts in the Mossy Wood and look for caves in the crevices of Cascade Peak. That's how I came across this place. It's hidden, built into the mountain. That's why it still exists, even though we as a kingdom have now spent generations trying to wipe away all traces of magic. A story for another day, I'm sure. In the end, it comes down to good luck. The witch who built this structure hid it well enough to keep it safe for more than a century."

Marianne took this in, picturing Jasper as a boy, looking for excuses to stay out of his home—just as Emory had. And what had Marianne done? She had left him alone with the very man he was trying to avoid. History repeating itself.

Is this what Emory would inevitably become, as well? The thought made her want to weep. Good, charming Emory, always desperate to please, using it for kindness—except when under his father's influence.

Marianne opened her mouth again, desperate for answers. "I did what you wanted. I left. Why am I here?"

A sad smile lifted Jasper's lips as he looked around the small stone dwelling. "For years, the witch tried to communicate with me, but I didn't understand. She was so lonely. You see, when magic was being erased from the world, she had the good sense to hide. But after years of holing up alone here, she created a spell and merged herself *into* the place she called home. When I first came upon this cottage in the mountainside, I didn't understand. I was frightened—but I was also curious. There seemed to be magic in the very walls, which was impossible, of course. Magic didn't exist. But that didn't stop me from investigating what turned out to be a haunted tomb.

"But really, it was no more terrifying than my own home. So I kept coming back, until I grew old enough that my absences started to become noticeable and my responsibilities made it impossible to get away. I regret to say, after that, I left the witch alone for a long period. It wasn't until I joined the council and learned the truth about magic's previous existence in our kingdom that I returned. I asked the witch in the walls about it, and she told me the long, horrifying story of her escape from the forces that wiped out the others of her kind. It's quite an interesting tale. Perhaps one day you'll learn it for yourself.

"Anyway, I resumed my relationship with the witch in the walls after that, learning more than anyone else in the kingdom—apart, perhaps, from Gabriel Glasslight—of magic and our true history. I came to terms with the fact that I would never have any magic of my own, but the witch is generous, and she was grateful to me. She wanted to share her powers, mostly in small ways—I can't draw too much attention to myself. Quietly, subtly multiplying my business, securing my connections. But tonight, she's agreed to something a bit more . . . dramatic."

Dread curdled in Marianne's gut. She watched Jasper throughout his speech, her face a mask of stone, unwilling to give him the satisfaction of seeing her panic. Her heart thumped wildly in her chest, so loud she was certain he could hear it. Bile rose to the back of her throat.

"I don't understand," she said as loud and clear as she could manage. "What is all this for?"

Jasper sighed. Both, it seemed from exasperation and, she almost thought, regret. "I'm afraid that simply walking away will not be enough, Miss Finch. Your fate has been written—Gabriel Glasslight saw it for himself—and the witch has informed me that fate is a tricky thing. The more we try and alter it, the more it comes speeding our way, threatening an even more violent collision. No. *Magic* is the only way to change things now. Even if I tried to *kill* you, there's no telling what would happen now that fate is involved. But don't worry, Miss Finch," Jasper added quickly at the look of horror on her face, "That was only to demonstrate exactly how powerful this is and why I was forced to resort to theatrics. As boring as it is, it comes down to nothing more than security. I was certain you wouldn't agree to accompany me to an isolated cottage to partake in a spell written by a generations-old witch. A spell to sever you from your fate—and Emory from his. A spell to swap your futures. Would you?"

"You could have asked," Marianne said furiously. "You could have tried."

Why did all the men around her refuse to simply speak with her about their plans? Why were they so certain she ought not to have a say?

Marianne didn't condescend Jasper's question with an y further answer; she only continued to scowl, trying her best to mask her fear. Why had she been so certain there was no reason to be wary? She knew Jasper was greedy and ruthless. He had put more than one village business under in his quest to build his own—nearly taking Ilya's down as well, thanks to his rumor.

If Jasper's simple merchant business was worth such destruction, then securing Emory's chance to work in the palace and study under the royal advisor must be worth going to the ends of the world.

Marianne tugged against the shadows holding her again, instantly regretting it. They tightened, making her cry out in pain.

Jasper looked at her with an eyebrow raised before his gaze fell to the shadows. "Ah. Yes. You'd be wise to stop struggling. But don't worry, my dear, this will all be over soon."

This will all be over soon.

Marianne lifted her chin. She stared him straight in the eye with as much defiance as she could muster. And yet . . . a small voice at the back of her mind lingered on the sentence.

Perhaps he was right. She had already agreed to relinquish her "fate," as Jasper referred to it. Maybe if Marianne could simply figure out how to settle herself, she could watch this nightmare play out with detached interest. And then go home.

A ripping sound distracted her as Jasper tore a sheet of paper from the notebook he was holding. It reminded her of Glasslight—ripping the page from his notes at the beginning of summer, handing Marianne her "fate."

How long ago it seemed now. And how wrong he was.

Jasper was reading it with a disapproving look on his face. His eyes flicked up to find Marianne watching him.

"Emory's," he said, holding up the notebook. "A lot of fluff, I'm afraid. I can't help but wonder—if the boy had spent less time studying and more time taking action, would we be in this mess?" He shook his head slowly, his eyes darting back and forth across the page, then lowered his voice, more like he was talking to himself than Marianne.

"No . . . I suppose not. 'Fate,' right? The witch said it's strong. Wily. But Emory was in the running for a *reason*. This will all be for the better. The spell will switch your fates, and then he can go about his business. He can secure his future."

"And me?"

Jasper looked up in surprise. "You?"

"Yes. What will you do with me at the end of this?"

Jasper chewed his lip, watching her thoughtfully. She couldn't decipher the look in his eyes, and it filled her with dread. Rather than answer, he turned away and crumpled the paper in his hand into a ball before dropping it on the stone ground. "There are three things required for a spell, did you know that? I didn't find any particulars on the workings of magic in Emory's notes, so I assume you don't know either. Apparently, Master Glasslight didn't feel that was a necessary part of your education. Luckily, you have me."

He cleared his throat and dropped another crumpled paper on the floor, this one a little farther from Marianne.

"The first is the spell itself. Of course, in order to craft such a thing, one must be fluent in the language of magic. It's an ancient and elusive thing, and as I've been unable to find any remaining books on the subject, for this I have had to rely solely on my witch. But she's very obliging—and bored, I'd wager, being trapped for more than a century.

"Anyway, the second thing required for magic, after a spell, is an offering." He dropped another crumpled paper on the floor, continuing the trail.

"From what the witch has told me, this can cover quite a wide range of things. Something personal, something organic—perhaps found in nature—something assigned a great amount of value by the individual himself or society at large—for example, money. I see in Emory's notes that Gabriel Glasslight mentioned the use of mythical creatures' bones. That seems quite clever, as they'd have traces of magic themselves, and offerings of the body seem to be of a particular potency. Bone, hair, blood—"

Jasper dropped the last paper in the trail leading away from Marianne and carefully placed the notebook at the end. Then, standing to his full height, he removed something from a shelf. He turned around and Marianne gasped as a glint from the lamplight caught the side of a dagger.

A dagger . . .

In spite of herself, Marianne leaned forward, an itch at the back of her mind tracing the etchings in the blade . . . connecting them to another time and place . . . something she had seen before . . .

It wasn't until Jasper twisted it that it hit her: It was the same weapon Marianne had been holding in one of the moving moments from the mirrored hall. The image rushed back into her mind: her dark hair escaping from her braid, her eyes blazing.

Her surroundings had mostly been unclear in the mirrors, unless they were particularly relevant, like Mrs. Pettlewhip in her bed or the city streets of Queensmont. So there was no way to be sure the mirror had been showing *this* dagger . . . this moment. Yet Glasslight had called them truths, pieces of her . . .

Understanding flooded her.

Glasslight's main method of magic was vision-seeking. Future. *Fate.* She could clearly picture the shadows stuttering in the lilac smoke of his pipe as he sat at his desk, lost in his visions—

Had he used that skill to craft a spell that showed Marianne and Emory pieces of their futures?

With a jolt, Marianne realized the dagger wasn't the only thing she had seen echoed outside of the mirrors. At the ball, when she had spoken with the queen, Marianne had made her laugh. Had Marianne been in her silvery dress? She had been so focused on the queen.

And Emory . . . she had certainly embraced Emory in the same passionate fervor she'd seen in those gilded mirrors, the image that had once frightened her. Even now, she could feel the ghost of his lips on hers, his strong arms pulling her close.

Three truths you will gain by summer's last rain . . .

That's what Glasslight's scribbled note had said. His promise of "fate."

Emory's kiss—her first truth. The queen's laughter.

And now, the dagger.

Three truths. Three pieces of Marianne's future. How many futures had been in that hall? How many could she still claim for herself?

How many did she want?

"The third thing magic requires," Jasper continued, cutting into her thoughts, "is . . . hm. I'm trying to recall the exact word the witch used. Effort? Yes, I believe that was it. She called it the 'power source' of a spell. Like the water for the mill or pedals and footwork your mother uses to activate her loom. Spell, offering, effort. Usually it's as simple as a few spoken words or the act of presenting the offerings. She said it's not unusual to bury them in the earth or, if the spell is meant to work on a person, to place them into pockets or sew items into clothing."

He raised his eyes to hers. Still, there was no malice or hatred. Only a grim, resigned determination. Almost reluctant. "Marianne, this gives me no pleasure, I hope you know that," he said, walking toward her. His footsteps were oddly muffled on the stone floor as he dodged the crumpled papers, as her ears filled with a buzzing and the world around her seemed to tilt. The whispers grew louder, scratching at her mind like nails.

Lifting the dagger, Jasper took a breath and bent down.

23

THE SPELL

MARIANNE SCREAMED.

In a flash, he grabbed hold of her arm. The shadows were still holding her tightly enough that she had lost feeling in her hands and feet as he pulled her shirt sleeve up and moved the dagger in his other hand into a fist, raising it high before bringing it down in an arc.

Marianne felt a searing pain as he slashed a six-inch trail down her left forearm. She screamed again for him to stop as dark red blood seeped forth, spilling down her bound arm and dripping onto the stone floor.

It pooled out, spreading. But before it had touched her shoe, something strange happened. The blood started to *sink*, disappearing into the stone, drop by drop, until nothing was left.

Marianne stared at the clean floor, stunned, until the eerie whispers grew louder, drawing her attention up.

To her horror, words started to form themselves on the longest wall—words, it seemed, that were made from her blood.

They painted themselves in slow, steady letters, one after the other, glistening ominously in the lamplight.

A spell.

It was in a language Marianne didn't recognize, though she supposed it must be the ancient one to which Jasper had alluded. The same one Glasslight employed.

She watched, frozen, as her blood continued to drip down her arm . . . drop onto the floor . . . appear on the wall.

"That's a good girl," Jasper said, almost soothingly. "Now, for the last bit. We're almost there."

He walked back over to the notebook he had placed on the ground, took the box of matches, and struck one, bending down until the tiny flame caught on the paper. Instantly, it curled and blackened, steadily erasing Emory's neat, painstaking words.

Jasper continued after that, relighting matches and then bending to light the crumpled trail of papers he had left, starting at the other end and moving closer to Marianne with each one, though the paper nearest to her was a few feet from the toe of her boot.

Marianne realized the shadows would almost certainly recoil from the flames, as they had done with the gold sparks in the forest. That must be why Jasper was taking his time, leaving the paper closest to her for last.

Her arm was in agony, the whispers and blood in the walls something out of a nightmare. If she could just wait, just breathe, it would all be over. All three pieces of the spell done.

She didn't want the future she was giving up anyway. And once this was over, Glasslight would almost certainly make it so that she wouldn't have to remember the terror. She could return to her mother's workshop and leave every piece of this summer behind . . . pieces of herself . . .

Three truths will you gain by summer's last rain . . .

What else had the note said?

A blood-pricked prophecy, a destiny plain.

She stared down at her bleeding arm. What more had it said? She had read it through several times, looking for clues.

Midst laughter and dancing 'neath gold-tinged stars,

Marianne recalled the ceiling of the ballroom . . . the thousands of painted golden stars . . .

A foe who will raze your bruised, blackened scars.

And then what . . . how had it ended?

But with a billow of courage where doubt once did dwell,
Amid fire and darkness, your spirit, at last, will swell.

The dagger sitting on the shelf where Jasper had left it reflected the flame of the nearest engulfed paper.

In that moment, a pull of dizziness sent Marianne lurching forward, bent double. The whispers in the walls grew louder still, becoming almost unbearable. The slide of blood down her skin, its methodical dropping on the stone floor, made her want to scream.

The spell was taking effect.

A whirl of images spun in Marianne's mind, grotesquely shrinking and stretching, their colors blurring. She *felt* Emory in her bones—his warmth and his ambition—and as his presence loomed she saw shadows of herself . . . feathering away. Moments she had lived and ones she hadn't. Her future and her past.

Laughing with Artie, walking the palace halls, evenings in the archives, teas with the seamstresses she had met in the palace basement, Glasslight's magic spinning around her like the pearlescent marbles from the mirrored hall, meeting citizens in cities she didn't recognize, staring out at the ocean with a smile, helping her friends in Silver Edge build a new watermill.

And Emory. His smile, his touch. His belief in her.

The memories and futures, all of them were Marianne's. Hers. Parts of herself that gave her energy and life and peace and joy. Parts of her that brought color.

And in that moment, she wanted every one of them so badly it became difficult to breathe.

Her gut wrenched as more of the pieces of her tore away.

A sob clutched her throat and Marianne looked up again, watching the line of tiny fires Jasper had left in his wake starting to snuff out, leaving only ash. And she felt as if she, too, was burning away, being stamped out, becoming nothing more than dust. Gray. An even more lifeless version of Marianne than the ones Ilya wove into her tapestries.

"Shhh . . ." Jasper soothed, when he heard her cries. "It'll be over soon. And the witch has crafted something more once it's done. Something I think you're already familiar with. I believe our friend Gabriel Glasslight would call it . . . what? Selective truth? You won't remember, you see? I can give you that, at least. Even after you stole my boy's future, tramped all over his spark. You give it back and I give you peace. A *gift*."

Marianne sniffed as tears rolled down her face.

So, she wouldn't have to wait and see if Glasslight would take her memories. Jasper and his witch would do that for him. If Marianne just sat and bled and gave. She didn't have to do anything at all as they took the parts of herself she had been trying to hide and ignore.

But she would.

The more she felt her futures draining away, the more certain she was she'd do anything to keep them. A bigger version of herself. Brighter. A version that *wanted*.

For the first time, Marianne realized that wanting alone didn't make her like Jasper. Emory wanted and dreamed and tried. And Glasslight, Artie, even Ilya. Her mother wanted more than anyone Marianne had ever met. Her dreams were simple by some standards and larger than life by others. And they didn't turn her into something ugly. They're what built her. What made her shine.

Marianne sat up straighter, breathing in the acrid smoke. As she shifted in the chair, she felt the bulge in her pocket from the silver thread, and she had an idea.

Her wrists were bound to the floor, pulling her arms down, but if she tugged just right, the shadows had just enough give . . .

The black tendrils wrapped themselves around her wrists more tightly when she moved, cutting into her already tender skin so that she had to bite her lip to keep from crying out.

But it was enough. Sucking in her stomach and pushing the very tips of her fingers into her pocket, Marianne was able to grasp the spool of thread and pull it free.

Jasper was almost to her now, lighting one of the last crumpled papers that made a trail from Emory's journal to where Marianne sat.

She'd have one chance. One aim.

He bent down, setting the tip of the match to the paper nearest her, and as he stood, his back turned away, Marianne took aim and dropped the spool to the ground, holding tight to the end of the silvery thread.

Her fingers trembled, and sweat slid down her back, mimicking the feel of the blood on her arm. She felt raw and ignited, terrified and sure.

Her eyes locked on the piece of paper engulfed in flames as the thread unspooled, snaking down . . . landing an inch too far from the paper.

She sank her teeth into her lip as despair filled her body.

It was getting harder to concentrate; the spell was ratcheting up, beginning to blot out her vision with nothing but colors and shadows of memories both past and future.

They were being steadily torn away.

The fire engulfing the paper was charring into nothing, leaving a smear of black on the stone. Then . . .

Marianne caught her breath as the flame touched another portion of the crumpled paper and reignited, just close enough to the spool.

For a moment, nothing happened. Then a tiny spark burst on the thread, and the spool caught, the flame licking along the length of string, racing toward her faster than she expected.

She forced herself to hold on to the thread, quietly urging it along as the flame rose and her skirts smoldered, her skin beneath burning.

She didn't cry out as she waited, waited . . . then the shadows circling her wrists seemed to screech, just as they had done with the gold sparks in the forest, and they were retreating, loosening from her wrists and ankles.

The thread singed her clothing, leaving livid red welts, but Marianne barely noticed.

Seizing the opportunity without a second thought, Marianne pulled herself free with as much strength as she could muster, though she stumbled through the haze of color in her mind as the sensation of something ripping itself from her center continued, leaving her tender. It felt like her very skin was being pulled from her bones.

Screwing her eyes shut, she put her hands to her head, trying to focus, hearing the thump of something—a knock? Her heart lifted. But then the thumping stopped.

Not a knock. Footsteps. Fingers wrapped themselves around her tender, bleeding wrists.

Marianne's eyes flew open.

Jasper stood in front of her, his eyes wild as he took in the scene, trying to piece together how she had freed herself.

Without a word, Marianne ripped herself free from his grasp.

She looked around, thinking of the image of herself in that mirror—the dagger. She needed the dagger! It was still on the shelf, reflecting the candlelight. She lunged for it, all but blinded by the spell, but with a thrill of triumph she felt her fingers wrap around the hilt.

Behind Jasper, she could see the letters spelled in her own blood sinking into the stone wall, rearranging themselves.

ALMOST FINISHED.

DON'T LET HER GO.

What would Marianne have thought if she had been able to see the full scope of horror surrounding herself in the mirror that day?

But the dagger was the only clue she needed, along with the unyielding determination she had seen in her own eyes.

Jasper noticed the words on the wall and grabbed at her, but she had the dagger now. He was between her and the door, though. And the spell was still working. Still ripping. Still taking.

Marianne made a stabbing motion, trying to aim low, hoping to damage nothing more than Jasper's leg, but as he reached for her, she misjudged, and the dagger went deeper into his flesh than she had meant, sinking into his thigh.

He let out a wail and collapsed to the floor.

Marianne's hand, slippery with sweat and blood, lost grip on the dagger as he fell with it.

She could barely see anything more than distorted colors and the shadows of flames throwing themselves against the bare stone walls. She could barely hear.

There was only her futures slipping away.

Marianne ran for the door, but as she reached it, the handle disappeared. The whispering grew louder still. The windows sealed themselves. Blood began dripping in steady streams, leaking from the ceiling and slinking down the walls.

Marianne whimpered. She could barely stand, barely think.

Jasper had clambered back up to his feet, but he was standing still, watching her with an unreadable expression, the dagger in his hands, dripping his own blood, which was likely mixing with Marianne's as it all fell from the cracks in the ceiling. He knew she was trapped. Knew there was no more reason to fight.

Desperately searching the room, her eyes landed on the matches he had left unattended.

She stumbled slowly away from him, keeping her weak gaze on Jasper as he watched her warily, unsure of her plan.

"You agreed, Marianne. You gave up your fate. Why are you fighting it? Look what this has come to! Look what you've done!" he said, gesturing to his torn and bloodied leg.

She could have laughed. Her wrists and ankles were an angry red, her legs burned from the thread, her arm streaked with blood, and her senses nearly gone.

Instead, she ignored him, pushing away the crowding colors in her mind until a plan started to form.

It was madness. If it didn't work, she would be sentencing them both to death, but she moved into the next room, looking for anything flammable.

The room was fitted with a decrepit bed and a moth-eaten blanket. Marianne ripped it free and moved back into the primary room, her feet faster now as she awkwardly ran for the matches, blinking too fast in her effort to focus her mottled gaze.

It didn't take Jasper long to figure out what she was doing. But by the time he did, she was lowering the flickering match.

"What are you . . . No!" he limped quickly toward her, the dagger held in front of him as Marianne touched the flame to the blanket

The fire spread quickly.

Struggling to stay conscious, she dropped it between them, watching as the flames leapt and thick black smoke filled the air.

The whispers in the wall turned into screeches. Shadows she hadn't realized were watching her from the corners wavered, rose, slunk away.

As fast as she could, Marianne grabbed anything that might catch and threw it on the blanket, watching the fire grow.

She pushed the chair she had been bound to against it, dodging Jasper as he came around the flames, dragging his injured leg, trying to grab her, sweat pouring down his forehead and neck.

All at once, the chaos in her head started to dim, the spell draining away.

The witch must have been focusing her efforts on putting out the fire. Marianne felt a wind lift her braid and noticed the flames around her start to diminish, almost as if the fire couldn't decide whether or not it wanted to burn.

Jasper seemed torn between fighting the flames alongside the witch or attacking Marianne. He made one more attempt at grabbing her, but as her vision began to clear, she was able to dodge him easily.

Then, suddenly, Marianne felt something snap, and she wondered if it was her futures breaking away. She froze, crying out, waiting, feeling, reaching inside herself.

She felt . . . whole.

Her thoughts cleared. Some of her strength returned, though her legs were still shaking, her head growing dizzy from the loss of blood. But in that moment, Marianne knew the spell had broken before it could finish. Her fates were still hers.

But still, the windows remained sealed. And the door had no handle . . .

BOOM. BOOM. BOOM.

Marianne blinked as the door pounded again, shaking in its frame.

Voices poured through, frantic, but she couldn't make out any words over the roar of the flame, the whispers turned to screeching. It seemed as if someone was throwing themself against the door. Over and over. There was more shouting.

Then the door blasted out of its frame entirely, and four figures stood silhouetted in the rain.

24
THE REUNION

EMORY CAME THROUGH FIRST. HIS eyes were wild, his wet hair raked back from his forehead.

"Marianne? Marianne!" When his gaze landed on her, something in his face changed. He took in her appearance—her blood—and then shifted his attention to Jasper holding the dagger.

He lunged.

Marianne cried out, barely noticing Glasslight and Artie and Ilya crowding into the small room. Marianne gasped at the sight of them all, each looking more murderous than the last.

In a flash, Emory had pulled his arm back. She heard yelling. Jasper's eyes went wide as he held his hands up in a sign of surrender, his lips open in explanation. But Emory wasn't listening, and the next moment his knuckles crunched against the bones of Jasper's face.

That's when Marianne's legs finally gave out, her vision going dark at the edges once again—not from poisoning or spellwork, but simple loss of blood.

Before she hit the floor, Emory caught her in his arms.

The fire was still dying down. The heat made their skin slick as he pushed Marianne's hair back from her face. Above her, sweat poured down Glasslight's dark skin as he looked around the room in a rage and boomed at Jasper.

The man cowered, holding the side of his face where his son had hit him. Meanwhile, Artie stepped up, coming only to Glasslight's shoulder, and joined in with a few choice words of his own, nearly bouncing in the air as he shouted obscenities.

And then Ilya was at Marianne's side, crying and speaking in soothing tones, touching her hair and cheeks.

Marianne lost track of time and details in the chaos that followed.

There was shouting, her head pounded. Hands grabbed at her, and she pulled away, crying out until Emory's face came into focus; she let him lift her. He carried her easily, murmuring words she couldn't make out as he took her from the burning mountainside cottage out into the rain; she buried her face into the warmth of him.

The drops splashed against her skin, soothing her burns and washing away her blood. He asked questions, but she couldn't focus. She saw only the fear and panic in his eyes and wanted to take it away.

She lifted her hand to his face and felt him wrap his arms around her, pulling her close.

"Marianne," he said, again and again, his voice choked.

"I'm all right. It's okay . . . it's okay . . ."

Her eyes shifted, and she saw Ilya just behind them. She saw Glasslight clap his hands together, his booming voice speaking that hissing ancient language; his tall frame cast tiny Artie into shadow as the old man continued to berate a bleeding, white-faced Jasper.

Marianne turned her face away and buried it in Emory's chest again. His shirt was soaked and sticking to his skin, but she didn't care. He ran his hands over her hair, and she clung to him, safe. And whole.

EPILOGUE

THE VISION

One Month Later
Gabriel Glasslight

GABRIEL GLASSLIGHT WAS NOT A patient man, nor was he a humble one. He especially didn't like being upstaged by an eighteen-year-old apprentice.

Luckily, he had developed not a small amount of affection for the girl. So when the visiting ambassador of the neighboring Kingdom of Grottland complimented her work on their most recent treaty—work that was supposed to be no more than a simple fact check but that turned into a crucial catch regarding a rather embarrassing oversight in regards to trade routes—Gabriel couldn't grumble too much.

He could, however, smile and take the credit himself, right?

The ambassador didn't *know* it was a Marianne Finch discovery. And after all, Gabriel had trained her, plucked her from a dreadful life of working her fingers bloody at some sort of antiquated weaving contraption, collapsing daily from the atrocious scent of noxious dyes clouding the workshop—and all with no magic in sight.

Gabriel shuddered at the thought.

But somehow, when he opened his mouth, what came out was (in quite a more affectionate tone than he meant), "Yes, I'm afraid you have my apprentice to thank for that one. Sharp as a needle, Miss Finch."

Well, she can thank her brains and *the fact that she can't seem to tear herself away from the archive,* Gabriel added to himself.

Not since the Leroux boy had taken up residence as Artie's most recent apprentice. Perhaps in the end it all came down to nothing more than raging hormones. For if his two proteges hadn't been hiding out between dusty shelves at all hours of the day, Marianne might not have come across the tidbit of Grottland land borders that made its way so effectively into the negotiation.

But he didn't say that bit aloud.

As if on cue, after wishing the ambassador a jovial farewell, Gabriel turned the corner in the hallway to find Finch and Leroux in the midst of a rather spirited embrace.

He cleared his throat pointedly and watched in satisfaction as the two broke apart as though they were recipients of powerful electrical shocks . . .

Oh, how Gabriel longed for electricity. He had spent days sketching out the workings after one particularly vivid vision, plastering the diagrams inside the wardrobe in the corner of his office—the one he kept closed when hosting visitors.

But although other worlds had already discovered the potent power source, Wyn wouldn't be lucky enough to welcome lightswitches for hundreds of years.

In the meantime, Gabriel supposed, he had his visions. And his magic. At least he didn't have to boil the water for his tea over a fire any longer. He'd worked out a spell for that one only a week ago, and it had already saved him several hours and quite a few headaches.

Marianne, whose blush turned an even deeper shade of maroon as Emory whispered, "I love you," quietly murmured the same, suppressing a smile as she turned to Gabriel and apologized profusely for the display.

He only scowled, pointing a finger into his office for their daily debriefing and lesson, smothering his own smirk as she scurried through the door.

For the most part, Gabriel had done away with his magical tasks since Marianne officially accepted the apprenticeship at the end of the summer. She had more than proved herself in that showdown with Emory's idiot of a father.

The man was no longer a threat, having been tried and imprisoned for kidnapping in their ridiculous excuse for a village. What was it? Silver Sludge? Gabriel could never remember. Though it seemed that watching flames engulf the witch's stone dwelling, incinerating everything flammable within the mountain cottage as her screams slowly died, had been quite the punishment in itself. That, and the punch his own son had thrown in his face.

Tracking Marianne and taking down the long-dead witch required quite a bit of inventive magic of its own, if Gabriel did say so himself. A set of spells he had spent every minute crafting, connecting, and adding contingencies and flexibilities to as he and the boy chased after Marianne.

It wasn't until they reluctantly stopped to rest the horses for the night that they discovered Artie happily sitting on the back of the carriage, his feet kicking as they dangled above the ground.

Apparently, after Glasslight's vision at the ball, he had overheard them discussing Marianne's sudden departure and Emory's worry at what his father was planning, and had taken it upon himself to join them for the journey.

After that, Artie rode in the carriage and learned Emory's part in deceiving Marianne in order to better prepare her for her role as apprentice, and her eventual leadership.

After three days cramped together, Artie had offered Emory a spot in the archive, refusing to let such a determined and compassionate mind go free, even if Gabriel was "too blinded by his smoke-filled visions to see the boy's potential."

Later, of course, he had proposed a trade: Marianne for Emory. Gabriel had flatly refused. Emory was impressive, but not even Artie knew what Gabriel had found in his apprentice—or the future she had in store. It seemed, however, that they all had a particular soft spot for her.

As such, coming upon her in such a state had been quite a shock to all of them, but especially Emory, who had thrown himself against the cottage with a fury that nearly broke the magically reinforced door without Gabriel's help.

Nearly being the key word, of course.

It had been Gabriel's magic that allowed them entry, and when Emory laid eyes on Marianne's blood and disheveled form, his father wielding a knife in her direction, the boy had become apoplectic, only holding himself together long enough to ensure Marianne was safe in the carriage with her mother—who had joined in on their hunt when they stopped at her workshop in their pursuit—before confronting his father fully.

Jasper was, by that point, on his knees in the rain, grieving the loss of his witch and the future he had tried and failed to secure for his son.

"I was in the archive this morning, after dropping my letter home," Marianne stated now, without preamble, as she sat in front of Gabriel's desk, bringing him back to the present.

"Of course you were," he muttered.

But the girl didn't hear, too busy launching into a diatribe about a cultural discrepancy she had read that likely explained the offense a foreign noble had taken from a remark about his nose.

As she pulled out notes and references, Gabriel tuned her out, his eyes drifting to the wardrobe with his sketches of future events and inventions. Ones, ironically enough, he wouldn't even be able to enjoy, considering the fact that magic interfered with technology any more advanced than the loom Marianne's mother worked on as she continued to build her fame, day in and day out.

Of course, that wasn't the only thing in his wardrobe.

The only two people in existence who had seen the full extent of Gabriel's visions were Gabriel himself and that scoundrel Jasper Leroux, after he so unscrupulously snooped through Gabriel's private effects.

Only the two of them had seen the drawings of locomotives, of television sets, of poodle skirts and a separate world with something called National Pizza Day.

And only the two of them had seen the penciled strokes of a familiar girl with a braid, her face aged but her almond-shaped eyes still blazing with the same intensity, and a gilded crown upon her head.

THE END

THANK YOU! PLEASE READ!

Dear reader,

I sincerely hope you've enjoyed your time in the kingdom of Wyn. Thank you so much for trusting me with your time, your heart, and your imagination.

The Futures of Marianne Finch takes place 50 years before the events of *The Secrets of Silver Edge*, the first full-length novel in *The Moonwell Archives*.

Because it turns out the village of Silver Edge is hiding some dark secrets, and it's up to Marianne Finch, along with a few new faces, to bridge worlds, untangle curses, and bring hidden truths into the light.

These books continue the heartwarming, whimsical, sometimes thrilling relationship-driven adventures that started here. I hope you'll continue the journey with me!

Sincerely,
Shirsten Shirts

ACKNOWLEDGMENTS

Thank you to my parents, my husband, my siblings, my children, and my extended family for your interest, your love, and your endless support.

Thank you to the incomparable Aubrey Sanders. Your talent is incredible, and your art is the perfect complement to my stories.

Thank you to Caitlin Dunn for your proofreading, your kindness, and your lifelong friendship.

Thank you to my beta readers: Madelyn Dyer, Grace Lanning, Evie Nelson, and Tamyrra Roberts. It means so much that you were willing to give your time and open your hearts to my words.

And thank you to my Father in Heaven for giving me the passion for storytelling and the support to make my dreams come true.

ABOUT THE AUTHOR

Shirsten Shirts lives in a 112-year-old cottage in Utah with her husband and four girls. When she's not writing, she loves reading, spending time with family, and bingeing early 2000's television. You can find her online at shirstenshirts.com and on Instagram at @shirstenshirts.

The Futures of Marianne Finch is her first published work.